TALK NOT AT ALL

The Thaed were biological engineers working with living materials as men work with ores and minerals. As surgeons they were unequalled anywhere in the known universe. They were an old race, and it was conjectured that they were responsible for creating and spreading life throughout the cosmos.

Anyone could come to the Thaed, who would then give them what they demanded…either in the way the supplicants wanted, or in a manner decided by themselves, whilst keeping to the letter of the demands.

But now they were decadent: sometimes they distorted flesh and bone to create creatures which were monstrous abominations—and for no other reason than that ii interested them to do it…

Another dynamic new collection from a Master of science fiction!

ALSO BY E.C. TUBB

Assignment New York: A Mike Lantry Classic Crime Novel
The Devil's Dictionary: Weird Fantasy Stories
Enemy of the State: Fantastic Mystery Stories
Galactic Destiny: A Classic Science Fiction Tale
The Ming Vase and Other Science Fiction Stories
Mirror of the Night and Other Weird Tales
Only One Winner: Science Fiction Mystery Tales
Sands of Destiny: A Novel of the French Foreign Legion
Star Haven: A Science Fiction Tale
Tomorrow: Science Fiction Mystery Tales
The Wager: Science Fiction Mystery Tales
The Wonderful Day: Science Fiction Stories

THE ATILUS TRILOGY

1. *Atilus the Slave*
2. *Atilus the Gladiator*
3. *Atilus the Lanista*

TALK NOT AT ALL

Classic Science Fiction Stories

E.C. TUBB

Edited by Philip Harbottle

WILDSIDE PRESS

Published by Wildside Press LLC.
www.wildsidebooks.com

CONTENTS

TALK NOT AT ALL

The Thaed were the engineers of life, working upon living tissue as the Earthly metallurgist fashions steel.

They say, those who claim to know, that when a man grows old death loses much of its terror and that, at the very end, he will welcome it almost as a friend.

It may well be so. The time will come, perhaps, when I will be able to make a personal test of this assumption. Until then I can only work on observed data and, working on such data, I have my doubts.

My data was the oldest and most terrified man I had ever met. The name was Gerald Lancaster and he sat facing me across a table in Lee Hung's Palace of Ineffable Delights which swung in a lazy orbit above the Earth a score of thousand miles below.

"I am a desperate man, Conwell," he said. "I want you to understand that."

Looking at him I could well believe it. He was tense with strain, a strain which had become so much a part of him that now it was difficult to see how he could ever relax. He was thin with an almost painful gauntness and his face, hook-nosed, lantern-jawed, was a finely engraved mass of lines. Sparse white hair straggled over a domed skull and his eyes, sunken deep in shadowed sockets, were wary and furtive, darting like trapped lizards, beneath shaggy brows.

"Desperate enough," he continued, "to have sent for you."

A goblet rested before me, a delicate thing of transparent porcelain gilded with the misty touches of a hair-fine brush.

A ruby liquid rested in oily quiescence within the goblet and the air above it quivered as if from heated vapour. I lifted it, swirled the contents with a turn of my wrist and held it beneath my nostrils. A heady vapour assailed my senses as I inhaled.

"Are you listening?" Lancaster sounded peevish, he was not used to having men do other than anticipate his wishes.

Again I inhaled and then set down the goblet; A troupe of winged Sirians danced into the open space above our heads and I watched their graceful gyrations as coloured lights sparkled from their iridescent scales. When the vapour had cleared from my head I looked at the man facing me.

"You sent for me and you are desperate," I said. "Two facts. Perhaps it would help us both if you were to tell me a little more. For example, what has made you desperate?"

"Fear," he said. "The fear of death."

"Assassination?" It was a logical question. A man as rich and as powerful as Lancaster would run the normal hazards. He dismissed the notion with contempt.

"I can take care of such matters," he said, and his eyes flickered to the surrounding tables. Men sat there talking to gaily painted women but the eyes of these men did not smile in company with their mouths.

"What then?"

"I told you. I fear to die."

"All men must die." I uttered the platitude without thought or feeling. It was obvious. All men had to die as they had to breathe. Lancaster startled me with the vehemence of his protest.

"Why, Conwell? Why?" His eyes burned like stars in the shadows of his brows. "Why must all men die? Because they have always done so? Follow that logic and what of progress? Men have to break away from what is and find new paths or we would not have fire, the wheel, the means to traverse the gulf between the stars." He controlled himself with an obvious effort, his doctors must have warned him against excessive emotion. "Think of me as a fool if you wish, but I prefer to be considered a pioneer. Someone has to be the first to cheat death. Why not I?"

The Sirian aerial dancers had gone; in their place was a coiling amorphous being from some wayward planet, who hung suspended beneath drifting lights and emitted sub-audible harmonies of nostalgic sadness.

"You have summoned the wrong man," I said. "I am not a gerontologist and I have small medical knowledge."

"You are a space pilot, a trader, a man of many parts and a man of dubious reputation." Lancaster caressed the delicate porcelain of his goblet. "I know all about you, Earl Conwell."

I could have argued, but I let it pass. Instead I concentrated on the poignant thrummings from the thing above our heads.

"Medical science cannot aid me," said Lancaster. "I have financed my own group of gerontologists for the past half-century but, apart from devising certain means to give a transient strength to this worn-out body, they have failed. All modern science has failed. All available science." He stressed the operative word and looked at me, his eyes strange in the drifting lights.

"Available?"

"Let us rather say, readily available." His hand caressed the goblet again and I could sense his hesitation. The lure of escape from reality into a dream-world induced by the heady vapours must, to him, have been a temptation hard to resist. He thrust aside the goblet so that it slid from the table and shattered into splintered shards on the floor.

"I will be frank with you, Conwell," he said harshly. "I want to contact the Thaed."

I said nothing. Those who know nothing about the Thaed use their name as an atheist uses the name of God, without thought or feeling or understanding. Those who know a little talk about them less and those who know more than a little, talk about them not at all.

"You heard me, Conwell?"

"I heard you."

"Then you know what I want. The Thaed can help me, I'm sure of it, and I want you to arrange a contact for me."

The amorphous thing had been replaced by a living ball of coloured light, hypnotic in its rhythmic pulsations. From it hummed a singularly sweet melody which seemed to hang and quiver in the scented air.

I looked at Lancaster, realising for the first time the extent of his desperation. He had reached the panic stage in which he would try anything and everything and give thought or consideration to none.

"Do you realise what you ask?" I said. "Can you realise it?"

"I think that I can." He was breathing fast now, like a man who has run a long way. "I have little to offer," he said, and now he was almost humble. "I have only money, but I will pay you what you want. You can have anything you want—if you will conduct me to the Thaed."

"And if I refuse?" My answer was written on his face. It would not be hard for Lancaster to avenge himself on any who crossed his will. "It will be dangerous," I warned. "More dangerous than you realise."

"I can only die," he said, and seemed to gain comfort from what he said.

To disillusion him would have been unkind.

* * * *

Memory is a treacherous thing. Seven years earlier I had fled from the planet of the Thaed vowing never to return. I had had my reasons, and yet time dulls memory as it dulls pain and fear and grief. I had suffered much and yet I had been fortunate also. Sometimes I felt the prickle of fear as I realised just how fortunate I had been.

And yet I was again approaching the planet of the Thaed.

There is an awful fascination in danger and the risk of destruction. And the greater the risk the more potent the lure.

Men have gambled their lives on the turn of a card or the spin of a revolver chamber and, winning, they gamble again. And they gamble voluntarily, without duress, and do not regard themselves as insane. So I could not, in all fairness, regard myself as other than sane for doing what I did.

I thought about it as I stared at the warp-drive. It sat like a fat spider in the heart of the ship, chuckling to itself with electronic power as it gathered the threads of space and time, spinning us along the web of the universe in a strange, half-real, half-dream dimension. We did not exist, the ship, the machine, those in the ship. We would not exist until our journeying had been completed and we were spat into reality in the environs of the planet of the Thaed.

It was quiet within the ship, aside from the chuckling of the drive there was no sound, and yet so softly did the woman move that I sensed rather than heard her as she came towards me.

"How is Lancaster?"

"Sleeping." Her name was Clitheria. She was tall with a well-developed body and hair which was like spun sunshine on a summer's day. Her skin was warmly saffron and her eyes were grey barriers to secrets no man has ever solved. She was Lancaster's doctor and, aside from he and I, the only person on the ship.

I remembered how I had protested when I had first learned that she was to accompany us.

"You're a fool for going, Lancaster, and I'm a bigger fool for taking you, but let us not add to our folly. The nurse stays behind."

"She is my doctor," said Lancaster. "I need her."

"But a woman. To Thaed!" It had seemed obscene to me then as it did now, but he did not, could not, understand.

"I trust her," he had said simply. "And she is willing."

I had argued no further. She was adult and, even though she was ignorant, it was not for me to educate her away from her desire. Once aboard she had taken charge of Lancaster while I attended to the task of plotting our course away from sanity. It was a long journey and it would have been easy for me to have allowed myself to be drawn towards her, but I remained aloof. A wise man does not permit himself barren emotions at any time and a man would be a fool indeed to fall in love on the way to Thaed.

"You are tense," said Clitheria, and her voice matched the perfection of her body. "Are we close?"

"Yes,"

"Curt, too." She sighed and stared at the chuckling machine. "I am not used to such curtness from men."

"Why do you go to Thaed?" The question burst from me despite all my resolve not to interfere. "Lancaster said that he needed you but that was a lie. He may have thought that he did but you and I know better."

"Lancaster is a sick and frightened man," she evaded. "It gives him comfort to be attended by one he can trust."

"He can trust me." I stared at her in sudden suspicion. "Does he?"

"He has to trust you." Again she was evasive. "But out here, alone, with a man he has just met—"

"He is a fool!"

"He is a man who has lived solely by reason of unremitting caution. Would you be trusting if you were he?"

"If I were he I would not be going to Thaed."

"Perhaps, but you are going nevertheless."

"For a million deposited in my name. For the threat of assassination should I have refused." I looked at her. "Were I a wise man I would have run the risk of assassination;"

"A live dog is of greater worth than a dead lion," she said softly. "And a million is not lightly to be refused."

"A million, on Thaed, is worth no more than the breath in your lungs." I moved from the chuckling machine and stared to where a spot of iridescent shadow rested on the wall. In normal space it was a direct vision port. Casually I said: "And you? How much is Lancaster paying you?"

"A quarter million." She said it simply, without shame or embarrassment. "The cost of a small hospital on Tanamasuri. There are still undeveloped places in our portion of the Galaxy, you know."

I knew that, and I knew of Tanamasuri also. I turned and looked at her with a new respect. It seemed odd that a woman with her grace and skill should choose to spend her life in the cesspool of the Galaxy. She noted my expression and, with a woman's skill, changed the subject.

"You fear the Thaed," she said.

"I—" My throat seemed to close on what I wanted to say. "I can't tell you." And it was the truth, the literal truth. I could think, yes. I could warn, yes. But I could not go into detail. She stepped towards me, halting with her face inches from my own and her hand, soft and almost caressing, touched my forehead.

"You mean it," she said wonderingly. "You are unable to tell me." The doctor replaced the woman and a glint of understanding hardened her eyes. "Conditioning," she said wonderingly. "Something has been done to your mind so that there are things of which you cannot speak." Her hand fell away from my face and her sharp, white teeth dug into her lower lip. "Now," she whispered, "for the first time, I am beginning to know fear."

"You do well to fear." My voice was harsh, unnatural. "It is not by accident that the name of the Thaed and the name of their planet is an anagram of death."

Then the machine abruptly finished its chuckling. There was an instant of twisting strain, the shadowed iridescence flickered from the port, and the cold stars flashed into being.

Below us the planet of the Thaed loomed against the glittering backdrop of the universe.

* * * *

It was vast, that planet, a great, featureless ball shielded by crimson cloud and swinging its lonely path around a dying sun. It was vast, but I knew that its density was such that its gravity was a little less than Earth normal. I felt sweat bead my forehead as, I stared towards it.

We had been seven. Seven men and a ship which was mostly junk, trying to scrape a living by dubiously honest trading among the scattered planets of the Rim. The natives had attacked on Fronden's World and then we were five. The pile blew while we were in warp and we'd emerged near Thaed with the ship a shambles and the crew more dead than alive.

We had landed on Thaed.

* * * *

I felt someone close to me and turned to find Lancaster at my side. He had rested during the trip but, nevertheless, he had aged.

His hands, thick-veined and with swollen knuckles, trembled as he rested them below the port.

"Thaed?"

"Yes"

"At last!" He breathed the words as if they were a prayer. His head tilted as he stared at something to the edge of the port. "Those?"

"Orbiting vessels of the Galactic Federation." I stared at the strange, polyhedron-shaped vessels which, I knew, enclosed the planet in an invisible skein of watchful alertness. One day, perhaps, Earth would be admitted to the Federation and would share the benefits and responsibilities of that vast civilisation. When that day came we would be truly adult.

"Will they stop us?" Clitheria's voice sounded in my ear.

"No. The planet is in strict quarantine to the Federation but not to us. They regard us almost as if we were dirty little children toying with undesirable pastimes." My voice must have echoed my bitterness. "Perhaps we are."

"And yet they find it necessary to quarantine the planet against their own?" Clitheria was sceptical.

"You do not understand." I gestured towards one of the vessels. "They are not there to prevent entry to Thaed but to prevent egress of the Thaed to the universe. They are a barrier around a cancer."

"If they fear the Thaed then why do they not destroy them?"

"The Galactic Federation believes in the sanctity of life," I said wearily. "It is the reason for our own continued existence."

I was tired of the discussion, and left them while I went to the control room there to signal to the orbiting vessels. The face of the monitor, as was usual whenever I made contact with a Federation vessel, filled me with the depression of inferiority. Not that he was arrogant, quite the reverse. But it was as if an aborigine should contact a civilised man who has already discarded as unimportant the things in which the aborigine takes pride.

I did not like to feel that I was an aborigine and I was not proud of what I was doing.

Then came the moment I had been dreading, the moment of no-return. Even now we could have left the vicinity of Thaed, slipped back into warp-drive and headed back to sanity. It would have been the wise thing to do and it would have given us stature in the eyes of the watching vessels, but even as the temptation came, so it died.

I signalled to the Thaed.

There was no response and I had expected none. The screen remained blank while my words dissolved into emptiness, lost in space and the regions below the crimson cloud. I had shouted into silence and had not received even an echo in rerurn. But, now that I had shouted, there was only one thing left for me to do.

I operated the controls which sent the vessel humming towards the surface below.

We landed on the shore of a vast, oily sea. There was no wind on this part of Thaed so that the thick, almost opaque waters rested stagnant beneath the crimson sky. A winged thing had guided us to this place. First it had appeared on the screen and then, almost immediately, before us, beating the air with tremendous wings, its razor-billed head pointed the path we had to take. We had landed and it had gone and now we were alone.

And yet, not quite alone. I spotted them as we left the ship and halted in my tracks, my hands catching at the others. Around us, tiny against the sand of the shore, rested a host of tiny winged insects. Smaller than bees and of the same colour as the sand, they were almost invisible. They surrounded us, crawling on the sand or lancing delicately through the heavy air before settling again. Clitheria tried to catch one, would have done had I not knocked her arm roughly aside. I stilled her protest.

"Don't touch them. They sting and their sting will paralyse."

"What are they?"

"You could call them the committee of welcome." I was not being humorous. "Should we try anything, then they will attack. Let us sit down."

"But—"

"We have a choice." I said gently. "We can sit down or we can lie paralysed and helpless. In either case we have to wait."

We sat and waited. Lancaster, naturally, was loquacious. He stared at the barren shore and the oily sea. He squinted up at the clouds and then distastefully at the watching insects. He was disappointed and he said so. And I knew why.

He had paid me a million for something he could have done for himself. There was no secret as to the location of Thaed. An autopilot would have both reached and landed on the planet. He had hired me to be his guide, his mentor, his agent to bargain with the Thaed for the thing he wanted. He had not realised that the Thaed operated under their own code. There were many things he had not realised. Discovering them would strain his sanity.

Something huge broke the water at the edge of the shore and slithered towards us. I seized both Lancaster and Clitheria as they started to, their feet and instinctively turned towards the ship. There was no safety in flight, the insects would see to that. There was no possibility of retreat either and for the same reason. Once a person landed on Thaed he stayed until given permission to depart.

"Relax," I said softly. "It won't hurt us."

It was hard to believe. The thing was larger than the largest whale ever to swim earthly oceans. Its colossal head tapered to a whip-like body; the undulations of that body providing its motion. The mouth, scant feet away from us and extending half-way down the grotesque head, opened revealing a cavernous interior ringed with teeth and fringed with ropy cilia.

"Enter," it said.

The unexpected is always shocking; the unnatural always terrifying, and the sound of that thick, bubbling, yet vaguely human voice made a mockery of the ordered scheme of things. I felt the others strain against my grasp so that I had to exert my strength to hold them.

"Enter," the thing said again, and its ropy cilia reached towards us.

I stepped towards it, dragging the others with me.

"No!" Clitheria fought to free herself. "No!"

"We have no choice." I stepped within the great orifice of tl mouth. "If we refuse the insects will sting us into paralysis and the cilia will drag us inside."

Darkness closed around us as the thing closed its mouth. Movement swayed us from side to side as it retreated back into the ocean. Then there was nothing but a gentle vibration from the spongy surface on which we stood.

I sat down, the others with me, and found that I could talk with a freedom impossible before.

"The Thaed are biological engineers," I said. "They construct things from living flesh and bone and tissue as we build from steel and plastic and stone. This thing," I slapped my hand down on the spongy surface, "is little more than a means of transportation. It is self-repairing, self-fueling, self-sufficient. Probably it can also breed others of its kind."

"And intelligent?" Clitheria asked the question.

"To a certain extent, no doubt."

"It spoke," she said. "It spoke in our own language."

I did not answer.

"It had the voice of a man." Lancaster spoke from the da ness. His hand found my arm, the old fingers digging into my flesh with surprising strength. "Conwell! It had the voice of a man!"

"You thought that it did. Any voice speaking in a familiar tongue would give that impression."

"No." He remained silent for a long time, so long that I wondered whether he had fallen asleep. "You haven't told all you know, Conwell," he said thickly. "Are you trying to trick me?"

"No."

"How can I be sure of that?" I detected a thin note of hysteria in his voice. "You've been here before. You—"

"Stop it!" The thin note of hysteria had risen and that, coupled with my own fear, resolved itself into anger. "I warned you against coming here, didn't I? Now that we're here we'll have to take what is coming. Whining about it won't make things better."

"Information would," said Clitheria quietly. "You could tell us more than you have."

"What can I say? What do you imagine I know of the Thaed? Do you want to listen to rumours? Shall I tell you that they take human bodies and human brains and build them into monsters? Is that what you want me to say?"

"Do they?"

"I don't know," I said desperately. "I don't know."

But I did know and I shuddered in the darkness as the thing in which we sat carried us towards the Thaed.

* * * *

I had seen them before and thought that I would never forget them and yet, when later I had tried to describe them, I found it impossible. How do you describe an attitude, an emotion, a sense of intangibles? But now, seeing them again, it seemed incredible that I could ever have forgotten.

I went to my knees before the tall, cowled figure and my head bent to the polished stone.

"Master," I said. "I have returned."

"Rise." The voice was emotionless, the voice of a machine. The word was without accent or inflexion yet it carried an authority I dared not question. I rose and heard the suck of breath behind me as the others noted my action.

We had left our living transport at the mouth of a tunnel drilled into a sheer wall of ebon stone. We had followed it to a small chamber and there we had waited until three cowled figures had stepped from an opening. My action and my words had been involuntary, something I could no more help than I could still the beating of my heart.

"Tell them," said Lancaster. "Tell—"

He fell silent, not because of anything said or done but simply because it was the thing to do. Men do not carouse in church nor do they shout in libraries. By the same token here was not the place for speech.

The cowled figures left the chamber and we followed. Again no word was said or gesture given; we followed because it was the thing to do. Our path led along winding passages of polished stone lit from above by drifting lights which, somehow, gave the impression of sentient organisms. They clustered just before our path, dispersing when we had passed, so that we were constantly attended by a cluster of drifting lanterns.

Clitheria's hand stole into mine.

It was quiet, only the sounds of our own feet broke the utter stillness, the Thaed made no sound at all. I watched them as we walked, tall, cowled figures, their coverings touching the stone so that it was impossible to see their feet.

Did they have feet? Did they walk on pads or glide like snails? Did they, even, touch the floor at all? To ask was to indulge in fruitless speculation. I had been here before but I had never seen a Thaed. All I had seen were their cowls which hid even their features. If they had hands and arms they remained hidden; faces and eyes the same. I could only guess at the nature of their bodies.

We entered a vast hall and Clitheria's hands tightened on mine.

It was big, that hall, so big that the drifting lanterns seemed like stars as they hovered above. The light was a soft twilight which revealed shape but not detail. Against one wall hung a tapestry, a thing of shimmering fibres and sombre colour. Things moved over it as if they were spiders spinning a web and, as I watched, one swung down towards me, strands streaming from orifices on its body.

It was not a spider.

I heard Lancaster suck in his breath and his voice, thickened with horror, rang in the stillness.

"God!" he said. "God!"

From the tapestry, from shadowed corners where distorted creatures toiled at their endless task of polishing the adamantine stone, from the upper regions beyond sight, came a thin, answering chorus, chittering and laden with the ultimate in despair.

Then silence resumed its sway, the stillness seeming even more tangible because of its breaking.

The Thaed had paused in the centre of the hall where stood a table of stone. Lights drifted down from the upper levels and illuminated our faces as we approached. I felt the edge of the table hit my thighs and halted, Lancaster to my left and the woman to my right. I tried not to think of what we had seen swinging from the tapestry. Silence mounted around us and then, suddenly, I knew the time had come to speak.

Lancaster felt it too and words tumbled from his mouth as if they were escaping from under pressure. I listened to him without paying attention, I knew what he had to say. Then it was my turn and I swallowed my fear.

"I want nothing from the Thaed," I stammered. "Once you gave me life and for that I am grateful. Now I have returned."

For a long moment I stood, the sweat starting on my forehead and then something, perhaps the impact of alien eyes left me and Clitheria began to speak.

"I am a woman who can never become a mother," she said evenly. "Radiation scars have rendered me barren beyond the aid of known medicine. I would be whole again."

I felt horror grip me as I heard what she had to say. All along I had suspected some deeper reason than Lancaster's money for bringing her to Thaed. I damned myself for not having questioned more closely, warned more strongly while there had yet been time. And yet I knew that it was a vain regret. I could not have uttered the words to warn her away, not then and not even now.

The silence closed around us again when Clitheria voiced her wishes. The Thaed stood as immobile as statues of stone and only the drifting lights above our heads showed signs of life. I became conscious of a multitude of eyes staring at us from the tapestry, the roof, the shadowed corners.

"You may speak."

Which of the Thaed had given the command I did not know, but that it was addressed to me there could be no doubt. For now I could speak as I had not been able to do before. But not in warning, in explanation.

It was too late for warnings.

"The Thaed are masters of life," I said dully. "They are biological engineers working with living materials as we work with ores and minerals. As surgeons they are, and have ever been, unequalled anywhere in the known universe. They are an old race, how old even they have forgotten, and it may well be that they were responsible for adapting and spreading life as we know it." I hesitated not liking what I next had to say. "It would even be reasonable to give them the credit for our creation."

I paused, wondering just how I had acquired this knowledge. Not for the first time I wondered just what they had built into my shattered body when I lay helpless in their chambers. A certain amount of conditioning that I now knew, but what else?"

"They are an old race and a decadent one. They have retained their manipulative skill but it has turned upon itself. They distort flesh and bone to create objects which have no real place in the scheme of things and they do this for no other reason than that ii interests them to do it."

And that was true, I had reason to know it. Words such as 'amuse' could not be applied to the Thaed any more than words like 'help' and 'hate'. But how could anyone explain the Thaed? How can anyone explain what it is that makes a man watch a line of marching ants and then, for no reason, either step on them or remove an obstacle from their path?

"Anyone can come to the Thaed," I continued. "And the Thaed will give them what they demand. But there is one stipulation. The Thaed will either give you what you want in the way you want it, or they will give it to you in a manner decided by themselves. In either case they will keep to the letter of your demands." The air seemed to have grown thicker around me. "Those terms apply to any and everyone who lands on this planet."

They did not understand, I could tell it from their expressions. Lack of imagination, perhaps, or a blind refusal to face the obvious. But they had to understand, it was essential.

"They can give me eternal life?" Greed shone in Lancaster's eyes. I glanced at the motionless Thaed.

"I don't know. If it is at all possible they will do it."

"That's all I wanted to know." He almost hugged himself with delight. He had forgotten what he had seen on the tapestry. Clitheria was not so blind.

"You said something about terms," she said, you mean?"

"I said that the Thaed would keep to the letter of your demands, but there are two ways of doing that."

She was beginning to understand. I saw her face whiten as she glanced at the things scuttling on the walls. Lancaster was still bemused by his dream of immortality.

"A million and a quarter it's cost me to come here," he said. "But it's worth it, every bit of it. If you give me what I ask," he continued, addressing the Thaed, "I'll give you five million. Ten! Anything you want!"

"You fool!" Anger boiled within me, rage induced by fear and perhaps something else. Was I, all unknowing, the instrument of the Thaed? Was this why I found myself beginning to hate the cheap huckstering of this money-mad dotard?

"Seven years ago I landed here in a wrecked ship with two companions." I forced myself to speak calmly, hard though it was. "We were injured, all of us, injured in the worst possible way. The pile had blown and what wasn't broken was burned and what wasn't burned was rotting with radiation sores. Anywhere else we would have died within hours of landing."

"So?"

"So we wanted to live and the Thaed gave us what we wanted. I was the lucky one, I lived the way I wanted to, in the shape and form of a man. The others—well, they lived, too, after a fashion. If you can call it living."

"The tapestry!" Clitheria shuddered as she stared at it. "That thing—?"

"Jud Owens," I said bleakly. "Once a man and now what you see. They showed him to me before I left."

"And the other one?"

"I don't know. I don't want to know. The only thing I am certain of is that he is alive and conscious and that every second of every day he prays for death."

"God!" Lancaster looked physically ill. I couldn't blame him. "Let's call it off," he muttered. "Let's get away from here."

"You can't." I was brutally frank. "You came here of your own free will but you will leave only by permission of the Thaed. And they will only let you go when the bargain is complete." I sought for a word to express my meaning. 'Bored'? It wasn't correct but it would have to do.

"They are bored," I said. "They have few diversions and are unable to acquire raw material because of the orbiting Federation vessels. They have to wait for fools like us to come to them."

"But you didn't suffer here," said Clitheria. "At least you are still a man and not a thing. Why you and not them?"

"I won the gamble," I said, and knew that I should have told them of this before. "There is a test, a competition, a chance of sorts and if you win it, then you win everything; if you fail, then you are their property, to do with as they will."

"What is the competition?"

"I don't know." It was the truth, I did not know. If I had ever possessed a memory of it, then that memory had been removed. I had even lost all memory of how I had been informed of the test at the time. Yet there was a vague recollection of a husky voice whispering to me from behind veils of darkness.

And, because of this, I acted like a fool.

"Master." My knees lowered to the stone and my forehead touched the ground. "I have made no demands and wish nothing from the Thaed. I returned with others. Is it your will that I must do as they?"

An aching moment of silence and then an unmistakable wave of negation. Elation was a living flame within me; I was to be allowed to go free.

I was tempted then, tempted almost to insanity, but I turned my head and caught a glimpse of the woman's face and read the horror that she was trying so desperately to conceal. And I thought of her as she might well become.

"Master." I grovelled when I would have preferred to stand and face the Thaed with the pride of my race. But I could no more help my actions than I could restrain the offer which blurted from my lips.

"Master. Let me take the woman's place in the chance proposed. Let her have what she demands without condition. Let me take her risk. If I win we both go free; if I lose she goes free and you do with me what you will."

"Earl!" Her instinctive cry of denial rang through the cloying stillness of the hall as a blade of light slashing through darkness. "Earl! No!"

I did not answer. Her cry died and stillness closed about us and the period of aching silence was longer than before. I seemed to sense communion between the Thaed and, had they been men, I would have had hope. Men would have known surprise, curiosity, a touch of wonder, perhaps, as to why one being should risk so much for another. But the Thaed were not men and their emotions, if they knew emotion at all, were incomprehensible in their alien strangeness.

Then it came again, that wave of utter negation, and the breath sighed from my lungs and I was coward enough to feel relief.

My offer had been refused and Clitheria would have to face her ordeal alone.

I did not look at her as they led us from the hall.

* * * *

I was alone in a Irving tomb an unknown depth beneath the surface of an alien planet and my thoughts were not easy to bear. We had separated when we had left the hall, each following a silent guide, Lancaster and the woman each to their respective chambers where they would be tested, examined, put to their ordeal, while I waited in my living tomb.

I looked at it again in the soft light of a drifting lantern, thankful that I was not wholly in the dark. The walls were of a soft, moss-like growth, the floor of stone. A raised portion, also moss-covered, served as a couch, aside from these the place was bare. There was no door but, just beyond the narrow slit, lurking at the edge of vision, squatted something I was glad I could not see. The Thaed needed no inorganic barriers when they had their creations shaped to serve their purpose.

Waiting is always hard; when tormented by imaginative speculation it can be refined torture. A thousand times I thought of Clitheria and the primeval urge which had brought her to this place. I thought of her as I had last seen her and then I thought of her as she might well be if fortune was against her. And I thought, how often I thought, of the machinery of the test she would have to undertake.

I had passed through it and yet I had no memory of it. That memory could have been removed and yet, pacing the narrow confines of my cell beneath the soft light of the living lantern, I began to have doubts. How can a man understand alien patterns of behaviour? It was possible that I had been tested without even knowing the nature of the test or how I had won. A boy could set a barrier before an ant and decide that, if the ant turned to the left it would be allowed to live, if to the right it would be destroyed. And if the ant turned to the left and so was allowed to go on its way how would it know that it had won a test? How could it know?

And, to the Thaed, men were less than ants.

Time ceased to have meaning in the soft-lit darkness. The smooth passage of the hands of my watch seemed divorced from reality and it was with something almost akin to shock that I found myself stumbling as I paced and the poisons of fatigue dulling my eyes and mind. I was exhausted, carried by nerves and tension to the brink of collapse. Or was it natural fatigue? Could there have been a subtle exudation from the surrounding moss? A vapour which dulled the senses, perhaps, a drug which quietened fear and induced sleep?

I did not know and had no way of telling but, as I sprawled on the yielding softness of the couch, it did not seem to matter. Nothing seemed to matter but the need for rest, for sleep, for escaping the torment within my mind. I slept and, when I awoke, I was a helpless prisoner.

The moss was more than normally, alive, that I had suspected; that it was a symbiote I had not dreamed. I opened my eyes and tried to rise and found that I could not. Tendrils fastened my arms to the couch, other tendrils laced across my chest, my legs, my throat. Something had grown onto my scalp and, as I lay in momentary terror, I realised that other extensions had penetrated into my body.

My terror did not last. It died in the moment of its birth and, in its place, came, a wonderful tranquillity, a sense of peace and termination of struggle. I and the moss were one. It would feed me, remove my waste, calm and soothe my fears so that, wrapped within its embrace, I could rest like a child in the womb. In return it took what little it needed and took it without harm to myself. Together we were greater than individuals apart.

And, somehow, it could communicate.

There were no words; words are clumsy things. There was no direct induction of concepts or visual images, our communion was more subtle than that. Instead I fell into a peculiar semi-dream state in which I seemed to see through other eyes and gain knowledge of things I had never been taught. Time and space ceased to be barriers so that, even while I knew my body was lying somnolent in the embrace of the symbiote, I seemed possessed of a strange mobility. It was as if I had left myself so that I stared down at my own figure and yet, at the same time, was aware of something looking down at me. It was as if I had merged with the consciousness not only of the symbiote but of other sentient organisms.

And, with that knowledge, came understanding.

I was a man and, as such, I had a conditioned attitude towards the inflexibility of life. Things were as they were and, to alter them, was something I could not regard with other than emotional reflex. A cripple aroused not only pity but a sense of revulsion. A man who was not whole was not wholly a man. Mutants, freaks, distortions of what was accepted as the norm, aroused hate and fear and disgust. Intellectually I could deny that; emotionally I could not. The inflexibility of life was, to me, a sacred thing.

But not to the Thaed.

Life, to them, was plastic, something to be adapted and altered, worked with as men work with metal, to be shaped and reshaped, built and torn down to be built again. I thought of an analogy; of the horror a race of machine-beings, creatures of geared limbs and mechanical bodies, of oil for blood and computers for brains, would experience if they saw how men tear apart their machines to rebuild them for other purposes.

To those robots, if they believed in the inflexibility of life, such actions would be obscene. To be subject to such treatment might well drive them insane. But, even if insane, their parts, to men, would still be of use.

I seemed to be drifting high above a table on which rested an amorphous being. From the edge of the table a line of tiny creatures, ant-like in their construction, marched towards and disappeared into an orifice in the colossal bulk. I knew that they would penetrate deeply into the creature and, at a selected place, they would shear away unwanted tissue with their razor jaws, digest it, smear exudations from their bodies on the wound so as to seal and heal it and, finally, their work done, would leave the creature as they had entered.

Life to work on life. Pygmies crawling in the heart of a machine, repairing and changing pipes, welding seams, replacing gaskets, reconnecting wires; work which a giant could do only by dismantling—killing—the machine. And the tiny creatures left no scars, required no clumsy surgery, gave no shock, caused no pain. They worked as beneficent bacteria work.

I thought always in analogy and, dimly I realised, it was because there was no other way in which I could understand— Understanding can only be gained by the use of familiar concepts; words only have meaning when aligned to previous experience. My symbiote was relaying information to me through the only channel it could utilise. But, to it, there was no difference between a man and a machine.

A machine can be built ten feet square and a hundred feet high. The same machine, the same parts, can be assembled ten feet wide by a hundred feer long and ten feet high. It will have a different shape but it can serve the same purpose. A sentient being is a brain fed by a body which may or may not have useful appendages. The shape of the body doesn't really matter, it will still feed the brain. A brain can be in a compact, easily carried mass or it can be spread out to cellular thickness; it will still be a brain.

Shape, unless it determines function, is unimportant. Function determines shape; so men build their machines and so the Thaed build their creations.

Kindness is a concept peculiar to man. Consideration, thoughtfulness, mercy, the Christian Law, all are peculiar to one race of beings, and the converse is also true. The symbiote was being neither cruel nor kind, thoughtful nor inconsiderate; to be either required emotions which the being simply did not have.

It showed me Clitheria.

She was naked, resting on a table, her body surrounded by the lines of marching, ant-like creatures. A peculiar vegetable-like mass of veined and mottled convolutions rested on her skull and I realised that she, like myself, had been merged with a symbiotic entity. Superficially she appeared unharmed and yet I knew that, deep within her, were tissues undergoing a major transformation.

The thing which sent me rearing against the confining strands was the awful doubt as to just what was happening to her. Had she won? Was she undergoing the relatively simple manipulation required by her demand? Or had she lost and was I even now seeing the first steps of her transformation?

I felt the lacing tendrils across my chest yield and part a little. My legs threshed and my throat swelled as I fought the thing which held me. For a moment black tides of madness clouded my brain and, from a great distance, I heard the sound of harsh panting and did not recognise the sound for my own.

The symbiote knew of the change in my blood. It discerned the increase of adrenalin, the glandular fluids released when a man lay wild with anger and fear, the rise in the temperature of the skin when he is under shock, the violent fluctuations of heart and respiration. It may also have discerned the disturbance in my emitted brain radiation. It adjusted its chemistry to quieten its host.

Darkness enfolded me. I lost the vision of Clitheria and, instead saw oddly shaped colours and weaving patterns of sombre brilliance Calmness steadied my heart and I ceased from the futile struggle against the tendrils which held me. I sighed a little and then, relaxing, I slept.

When I woke I was not alone.

The Thaed stood just within the narrow portal. Three of them, never had I seen less than three together, never more, always three. Their cowls made them seem taller than they must really have been and the drifting lantern cast their shadows in shifting pools on the polished stone. Around me I could feel the embrace of my symbiote withdrawing from my body, slowly, easily. With an impression almost of regret the living moss absorbed its extrusions and I was free to rise.

"Master." Again the genuflection, knees to the stone and head bowed to the ground. Why had they built this conditioned reflex into my body? Was it a precautionary measure? It seemed hardly likely that they would need such protection and, surely, it could not have been for any personal satisfaction they may have experienced at being so saluted. Once again I felt the baffling impossibility of trying to understand the motives of an alien race.

I rose to my feet, feeling an unnatural litheness when I had expected to be stiff and perhaps a little weak after my imprisonment. How long I had lain in the embrace of the moss I had no way of telling, but it had not been a short time, of that I was certain, and a little weakness would not have surprised me. But I was not weak. I was agile and felt stronger than at any other time in my life. The symbiote had taken good care of its host.

I followed the Thaed as they left the chamber and was pleased that whatever they had left to watch over me was no longer in attendance. I could not see it but I knew that the Thaed were far from defenceless: The creatures they fashioned would be within easy distance for both offensive and defensive measures. And yet, even while I thought about it, the concept of attacking the Thaed dissolved from my mind. It was one of those things which just could not be.

Together we walked in the stillness and, of the four, I was the only one making sound.

The passage led a winding path past narrow-doored chambers into which I had no desire to peer. The drifting lanterns clustered in ghostly attendance as we progressed and I had the impression of watching eyes. The Thaed went before me and the temptation to look over my shoulder became almost overwhelming. If we had not reached the hall when we did I would have yielded to that temptation.

Instead I stared at the thing on the table.

It was a cone, a foot in height and the same in diameter at the base. It was of a dull scarlet in colour and was utterly featureless. It could have been made of metal or glass or even of plastic, but I knew that it had been manufactured from none of these. There was an aura about it, an intangible something which gave the impression of life.

I was looking at one of my companions.

I think my sanity was saved then by the conviction that it could not have been Clitheria. She had wanted the power to become a mother and this thing obviously could not breed. What it could do was beyond my conjecture. Why it had been fashioned at all was past comprehension. A man would use it as a door-stop, perhaps; a giant for a paper-weight. The Thaed had constructed it for a whim, an exercise in their art. Their reasons were known only to themselves.

I followed them out of the hall, away from the tapestry on which things which looked like spiders spun in endless industry, away from the table of polished stone and the thing which rested on that table. The human brain locked in the cone-shaped body. Away from Lancaster who had wanted eternal life and who had received what he had demanded in a form to which death would have been a welcome relief.

We came to a chamber in which I seemed to catch a hint of sea-smell and there I was left to wait with a pounding heart for what was to come. I saw the clustered lights down the passage. I saw them draw closer and I saw the tall, cowled figures beneath those lights. And I saw who was following them, walking as if in a dream. Together they entered the chamber.

Clitheria bowed in utter subjugation. "Master."

She was well, I saw that in the first glance. She was woman, all woman, whatever had been her test she had won her chance. She genuflected before the Thaed and, even as she did so, my mind spun with questions. Why, Master? Why always the singular when addressed to the plural? Why not, Masters? And why, why had I never seen more than three?

Were they the very last remnants of a dying race?

The questions died in my mind as Clitheria rose and stood at my side. Together we stood waiting; two children in a world so adult and wise with time that we could never hope even to understand the smallest part of it. And, like children, we received our permission to depart.

"Go."

We bent as one. Our knees hit the polished stone, our foreheads touched the ground and our voices blended into a muted chorus.

"Master."

Then we turned and walked to our freedom.

* * * *

Tanamasuri is not a pleasant place; some have called it, with reason, the cesspool of the Galaxy. But to Clitheria and me it is home.

To the small hospital, built and maintained by Lancaster's money, come the disease-ravaged creatures of a dozen worlds. They come for medical help, for drugs to ease their torment, for hope when there can be no comfort and for comfort when there can be no hope.

We are respected, Clitheria and I, though at times I feel that that respect stems more from fear than from true regard. Whatever the reason, we are never molested, our hospital is never robbed, our staff walk the streets of Tanamasuri as they would walk the streets of any civilised city.

There is a girl, so much like her mother that it hurts my heart to see them together, and a boy who, so people tell me, is the image of myself. We are happy enough, Clitheria and I, in our work and our children and our love for each other. But sometimes, when the hospital has been busy and medical science shown again for the crude, fumbling thing that it is, I catch her expression and I know of what she is thinking.

And sometimes, when we dine out, and I watch the strange, amorphous creatures provided for our entertainment, I grew thoughtful and memory becomes an enemy.

We talk then. Talk of gay, inconsequential things, of the routine of the day and the progress of our children and, even, of the distant past.

But of the Thaed we talk not at all.

SUBTLE VICTORY

He walked into the tavern at midnight, a tall man, incredibly thin, shabbily dressed, with a skull-like head and two black thumbprints for eyes against the white dough of his face.

He stood, swaying a little, his thin streak of a mouth tight-pressed, almost comic, almost ludicrous, but somehow utterly serious and totally disturbing.

An odour hung around him, the smell of a dozen different gutters, the taint of alien soil, and a thin, sickly sweet scent, like a tomcat, an eucalyptus tree after a warm rain, like the smell of rotting flesh.

For a moment he stood, staring directly before him with his dull eyes huge against the bone-whiteness of his face, and as he stood, the normal sounds of midnight revelry died, died, and made room for something from the stars, alien, unknown, and yet at the same time familiar and horrible.

Men stopped drinking and stilled their raucous laughter. Women stared, shuddered, then stared again, forgetting to worry about their make-up, their escorts, or their rent. In one corner a juke box, previously ignored, boomed with strident melody, trying hard but waging a losing battle with the muted thunder of the space ships blasting from the nearby rocket port; then he moved, and the spell was broken.

Laughter rilled from painted mouths and twisted lips. Jowls shook and paunches quivered, and the tinkle of ice and spoons and pendant jewellery rose again in the frenzied noise of make-believe-we're-having-a-good-time. Smooth shaven, well-dressed men with fixed smiles and bulging muscles moved purposefully through the crowd. They nodded, apologized, slipped deftly beside the stranger and reached for his skeleton thin arms.

Somehow they just missed touching him.

He moved. Like an animated collection of bone and skin and rag, he moved. Stiffly, painfully, as if operated by invisible wires handled by a clumsy puppeteer, he plunged towards the bar, his dull eyes unblinking in his bone-white face, his arms swinging as if made of wood, his legs jerking as if he had forgotten that he had knees.

He bumped into a table. He bumped into a fat man and then he bumped into a thin woman. He didn't seem to notice the obstructions, but veered a little, his arms and legs still moving in the same deliberate rhythm, and so he came to the bar.

And Jeff Walker stared at him in horror.

Jeff Walker, thirty years old, tall and supple with the bloom of perfect health, a glass in his hand and money in his pockets, killing time before his next assignment. He stared at the thing pressing against the edge of the bar and felt his stomach twist and writhe in shocked understanding.

"Commander Peters," he blurted. "When did you arrive?"

No answer. The thing still leaned against the bar, his dull eyes fastened on the rows of bottles and his claw-like hands trembling as they rested on the polished woodwork. A man slipped between Walker and the commander. A smooth individual, a smiling man who had forgotten how to laugh. He rested one hand on a thin shoulder and muttered quick words.

"Come on, tramp. Outside."

He might have been addressing a corpse.

A faint red tinge touched the smooth cheeks and the hand tightened, the thick fingers grinding against bone.

"You heard me, bum! Outside!"

"Wait!"

Jeff stepped between them, knocking the man's hand away from the skeleton shoulder. He smiled at the flash of anger in the bouncer's eyes and jerked his head.

"Beat it! This man is a friend of mine."

"Friend?" The bouncer wrinkled his nose and hesitated, his big hands flexing at his sides.

"You heard me, or would you rather this place be boycotted by spacemen?" Jeff smiled and coolly beckoned to the bartender. "Whisky—bring a bottle."

"Yes, sir."

Deftly Jeff stripped off the seal and poured a full five ounces of the smokey fluid into a glass. He set it before the white-faced man, and snapped his fingers before the staring eyes.

"Drink up, commander. Drink deep."

Obediently the man lifted the glass, tilted it, set it down empty, the liquor seeming to have less effect than pure water. Jeff poured a second five ounces, then turned to the bouncer.

"Listen, stay here, keep feeding him liquor. I'm going to make a videophone call, and I want you to look after him while I've gone."

"Yeah?"

"Yes." Impatiently Jeff reached for his wallet and flashed his identification. "Now remember, don't excite him, don't deny him anything he wants, and above all, don't hurt him."

"Sure," the man said sarcastically. "I'll wet-nurse him for you—like hell!"

"You'll do it and like it, or I'll have you for obstructing the law." Jeff stared at the man, his eyes narrowed against the firm hardness of his face.

"Maybe you didn't understand. I'm telling you, not asking. That man is now under the protection of the government. I'm going to get an ambulance. All I want you to do is see that none of your friends decide to toss him into an alley."

"I don't like it," said the man. "He stinks."

"So what?"

"So the boss won't like it. The customers don't like it. *I* don't like it."

"Then lump it," snapped Jeff, and turned away.

Silently the thing that had once been a man lifted his glass, emptied it, set it down and stood waiting.

Irritably the bouncer reached for the bottle.

It took ten minutes for the ambulance to reach the tavern and in that time more than half the revellers had glanced at their watches, stared at the parody of a man at the long bar, then headed for the night and the clean stars.

Ten minutes changed a roaring tide of human merriment into something like a wake, and with the emptying of the tavern the tall thin man at the long bar took on a new and subtle importance.

Jeff nodded to the bouncer, now white-faced and twitching. He glanced at the two empty and one freshly opened bottle, and turned to the man who had entered with him.

"Was I right, doc?"

The doctor grunted, sniffed at the sickly sweet odour, touched the dead-white skin, stared at the dull eyes, and bit his lips.

"Looks like it, Jeff." He thumbed his hat back on his head and frowned. "How did he get here? You know him, you say?"

"Yes. Commander Peters. The last time I saw him was on Venus. He was in command of the garrison there, but that must have been six months ago."

"I see. Was he like this then?"

"No. Nothing like it." Jeff stared at the emaciated figure of the commander and shuddered. "Peters was about thirty-five, not over muscled but in good condition, a regular soldier and proud of his appearance."

"Something's altered all that," said the doctor. He sighed, glanced around the empty bar, and looked at the dead men on the counter.

"Did he drink all this?"

"Yes. I thought it best to feed him alcohol. From what I saw he'd reached critical point, ready to cut loose at a wrong word. The only thing I could think of was to slow his reactions with whisky."

"You did right," said the doctor. He shuddered as he stared at the dead eyes in the bone-white face. "We were lucky at that. If you hadn't been here, there's no knowing what might have happened." He sighed and jerked his head at the twitching bouncer.

"You'll find an ambulance outside. Tell the men to bring in the stretcher."

The smoothly shaven man turned away, then hesitated, his eyes fastened on the tall thin figure standing against the long bar. "What's the matter with him, doc?"

"Don't you know?"

The bouncer swallowed and shook his head. "I've seen drunks and I've seen dopes but I've never seen a thing like that."

"You have now," snapped Jeff curtly. "Get the stretcher." He waited until the man had left the room, until they were all alone against the long and deserted bar, then he whispered quietly in the doctor's ear:

"A new one?"

"Looks like it," murmured the doctor. "Hard to tell just yet, but he doesn't show the usual symptoms. That smell—I don't like it. And look at his eyes, his skin; a man shouldn't go like that within six months."

"Shall I order a quarantine?"

"Yes. Seal the place and, track down everyone who was here tonight. I don't think it's an exotic disease, but we can't be too careful." He glanced up as two men entered bearing a folded stretcher. "Right, be careful with him, but don't let him touch you more than you can help."

"Leave it to us, doc," grunted one of the men competently. Together they opened the stretcher, rested it on the floor; stood one to each side of the silent man at the bar, and with one concerted motion lifted him and placed him on the stretcher. Rapidly they locked the retaining bars, and picking up their burden, left the room.

The doctor nodded to Jeff, sighed again, and followed them out.

"You going to lock the place?" A small man with a worried expression stood beside Jeff. He wore a faded carnation in the lapel of his dull black jacket, and his breath carried the subtle odour of chlorophyll.

"For a while," said Jeff.

He stared at the man. "You the owner?"

"I bought the place a month ago; now this has to happen." He snapped his fingers at the bartender.

"Drink?"

"Whisky."

"Bring a bottle," ordered the small man. He gnawed at his lower lip. "Must you lock me up?"

"What else?" Jeff shrugged, feeling a slight sympathy for the man, yet knowing there was no alternative. "It won't be for long, just until we decide whether or not that character had a contagious disease. You can speed things up if you'll let me have a list of all the people here tonight."

"How can I do that?" The small man poured golden fluid from the bottle the bartender set before him and glanced up at Jeff. "Some of them I know, the regulars, some of the girls, but the rest are drifters. Spacehands from the rocket ships, sightseers touring the space port. I couldn't even guess who comes in here at night."

"That's a pity." Jeff sipped at his glass and rolled the liquor around his tongue. "You'll just have to pray that we don't find anything serious."

"It's a hard life," grumbled the little owner. "What with one thing and another, the protection I have to pay, the graft, and now a, zombie comes in and scares all the customers away." Disgustedly he swallowed his drink and gestured towards the bottle. "Help yourself. I've got things to do."

Jeff nodded, watching the small man as he walked across the floor towards his office. The jukebox boomed, then abruptly fell silent as someone cut the power, and the muted thunder of a distant rocket ship echoed in the silence.

It was all wrong, thought Jeff tiredly. Such things shouldn't happen here. On Venus, yes. On Mars, yes. On the raw frontiers of space where men lived on a razor's edge and rubbed shoulders with the unknown, such things could happen, but not here, not on snug little Earth.

He tilted the bottle, watching the golden liquor gurgle from the narrow neck and into his glass, thinking of how Peters had swallowed whisky as if it had been water. The bartender moved along the counter towards him, swabbing and clearing away the empty glasses, his broad face impassive and expressionless.

"Finished, Mac?"

"Not yet." Jeff pushed the bottle towards the bartender. "Have one."

"Thanks." Deftly the big man poured a shot and lifted the glass. "Mud in your eye."

"Have another?"

"Thanks, but not this time." Silently the big man swabbed the bar, then glanced at Jeff with calculating eyes.

"You knew him, didn't you?"

"Who?"

"The lunk who came in here, the one who scared away our trade."

"Yes."

"I thought so. Standing behind a bar the way I do, a man can see most of what goes on. I could see that you knew him, and you weren't i the only one."

"Not the only one?" Jeff forced himself not to display his excitement. "Someone else knew him?"

"Yeah. A spaceman by the look of him, a stranger here, but he knew the lunk all right. I watched him. For a moment I thought that he was going to pass out, then he left."

"A stranger, you say?"

"That's right. We get them in here all the time."

"I see." Jeff slipped from his stool and nodded at the bartender. "Finish the bottle. Goodnight."

"Goodnight."

Silently the big man swabbed the bar. He rubbed and rubbed, and when Jeff left he was still rubbing.

But there are some things, Jeff thought, a man just can't rub away.

Memories for example.

The memory of a tall, straight soldier, a man who had dedicated his life to the military, and as such considered personal appearance as of prime importance. Peters was such a man. Once he had been immaculate, his uniform neat and, spotless, the insignia bright and shining. Now...?

A tramp. A shattered parody of what he had once been, stinking with the filth of assorted gutters and smelling of rotting flesh and stale sweat. Something had happened to him, something within the past six months, something which had turned him into a travesty of a man.

Jeff wondered what that thing had been.

Disease? Maybe. The colonies were still too new, the frontiers still too wide for everything to be known about them. Perhaps some new virus, some germ or bacteria, a new affliction.

Drugs? Maybe, but Peters hadn't been the kind of man to experiment with drugs, and yet men did strange things when isolated on the fringe of civilisation.

Jeff shrugged.

Tomorrow would tell.

* * * *

The Department of Exotic Drugs and Diseases occupied a small section of one of the wings of the main hospital, and fought a constant battle against ignorance, lack of funds, vested interest, and plain hate.

Passengers from the space ships didn't like to be vetted before being allowed to leave the rocket port. They didn't like to have their souvenir plants and extra-terrestrial organisms confiscated, and they didn't like the strict search for forbidden drugs. Importers chafed at the necessity of obtaining clearance certificates for their cargoes of alien fruits, bulbs, spices, and other goods, and no one in living memory had ever admitted that the cold logic behind enforced quarantine had something to commend it.

Jeff thought of these things as he walked across the concrete surrounding the huge hospital. As an established member of the department he had met his full share of contempt, hate, disgust, and cold arrogance. He had even met bribes, offers of graft, and vague promises of favours to come with the same easy indifference.

He knew just what could happen if the department ever relaxed its continual vigilance.

A man nodded to him as he entered the hospital. A nurse smiled at him, and a fat importer scowled as he passed. Three worried looking people glanced up from where they sat on a bench against a wall, and a little girl turned shyly to her mother. Then he stood in the outer office and waited impatiently while the receptionist operated switches on her intercom.

"Room five thirty-three," she smiled. "The doctor left word that you were to go right in."

"Thanks," he smiled, then jerked his thumb towards the vestibule. "There's a little girl out there; what gives?"

"Little girl?" The receptionist frowned, then nodded as memory returned. "I remember now. She's here with her mother; they're waiting for the verdict on her father. He contracted a tumourous growth while working on the new project on Mercury."

"Serious?"

She shrugged. "Maybe, maybe not. The results should be here soon. Personally I hope that it isn't. The poor little thing has only seen him once, a short while at the rocket port through the glass barrier before we vetted him." She sighed and operated the electric lock on the inner door. "See you soon?"

"Maybe." He smiled, shrugged, and passed into the main section.

The doctor was waiting for him in five-thirty-three.

He looked tired, his old features lined and grey in the morning light, his eyes red with strain and sheer fatigue. He smiled as Jeff entered the room, and moved away from the silent figure on the narrow cot.

"How is he, doc?"

"Bad, Jeff, very bad."

"Is it a new one?" Jeff glanced at the limp figure of Peters as he voiced the constant dread of all who worked at Exotic—a new disease, an infectious disease which would sweep through the un-resistant population. Slowly the old doctor shook his head.

"I don't think so, Jeff; at least I can't trace any symptoms of malignant organisms, but in a way it is something new."

"Dope?"

"Perhaps."

"Aren't you sure?"

"No." Wearily the old man stared at the silent figure on the white cot. He sighed, and when he spoke it was as if he spoke to himself rather than to the young man at his side.

"From all appearances the man has almost starved to death. He is horribly emaciated. There isn't a vestige of fat left on him, and even his muscular tissue has shrunk to a point where it is doubtful if he will ever regain full use of his limbs."

"What could have caused that, doc?"

"Starvation. Simple lack of food. Such cases were common enough during the past wars, and even now we stumble across them when a crew has been drifting for a long time in a wrecked rocket ship."

"But Peters wasn't wrecked," protested Jeff. "He was free, at liberty to buy or beg food at any time. How could a man deliberately starve himself almost to death?"

"I know that, but the fact remains, he obviously hasn't eaten for a long time."

"I see." Jeff stepped to the side of the bed and stared down at the ravaged features of the man he had once known. Deliberately he flipped back the single sheet, then hastily replaced it.

"What...?"

"The physical condition?" The old doctor shrugged. "Another mystery. From the state of him I would say that he has neither taken a bath or even removed his clothes for several months at least. A nail had worked through the sole of his shoe, penetrated the skin, caused a running sore, a sore which had gangrened. I had to amputate the foot. Another two days and it would have been his leg, three days and death would have been inevitable."

He stared down at the hollow cheeks and pasty white face.

"The smell of course was mostly dirt, and sweat, but analysis of the dried perspiration shows definite traces of some alien compound. And whatever it was caused Peters to forget he was a man obviously contained some energising element."

"What makes you say that, doc?"

"If he hasn't eaten for as long as he didn't remove his clothes, then he would have been dead a long time ago. Something has provided sufficient energy to enable him to last this long." The old doctor sighed again and turned away.

"We neutralised the alcohol you fed him, of course, and gave him intravenous injections of glucose, saline, and liquid nutriment."

"Naturally. Will it do any good?"

"Maybe. It's hard to say so soon, but with luck we may be able to pull him through. There's just one other thing."

"Yes?"

"He bears the scars of recent surgery, on his back. It would seem as if someone operated on him, a double operation; once to lift a flap of skin and muscle, and again later the same operation was repeated." The old man stared at Jeff. "What do you make of that?"

Jeff shrugged. "Do you want a wild guess, doc, or would you rather wait and hear all the information?"

"You've uncovered something?"

"Yes. Peters landed at Tycho station two months ago. I've checked with the military. As usual they didn't want to talk, but I convinced them it was essential that we should know as much as possible. He resigned his commission and returned to Earth, landing as I said, two months ago."

"Resigned his commission? Why?"

"I don't know," said Jeff slowly. "I knew Peters. He was a professional soldier, been at it all his life. Whatever it was made him resign must have been pretty important to him." He bit his lips and frowned down at the silent figure on the bed.

"What made him do it?" he whispered. "What made a man like Peters, a professional soldier, commander of the Venusian garrison, a man with more than his share of pride and ambition, throw up everything he valued and return to Earth to rot in the gutter? Why?"

The old doctor didn't answer, the thing on the bed didn't answer. For a moment silence hung heavily in the tiny room, then the inter-com hummed its urgent signal.

Irritably Jeff closed the circuit.

"Yes?"

"Who is speaking, please?"

"Walker, Jeff Walker."

"Are you alone?"

"The doctor is with me. Why do you ask?"

"Will you both go at once to the conference room, room seven-eighty-nine. You are expected; do not delay."

The metallic voice fell into silence, and Jeff slowly opened the circuit.

"Conference room!" He stared at the old doctor. "Something must be brewing, something vital. Let's go."

Together they left the silent room. Behind them, on the narrow white cot, the ruin of what had once been a man opened heavy lidded eyes, and stared dully at the painted ceiling. After a long while he closed them again, then rested quietly, lost in the dim regions of his own secret thoughts.

Three men sat in the small conference room. Three men with old tired faces, red sleepless eyes, and deep lines traced in the flesh of their sagging jowls. They were tired, these men, tired with the ceaseless battle to keep Earth sweet and clean, free of alien disease and exotic drugs. They wore their uniforms on their sagging features. The deep lines were their battle scars; their red eyes and agile minds their only weapons.

One of them gestured towards chairs as Jeff and the old doctor entered, then pressed a button, sealing the room from outside interference.

"I'll make this brief," he said in his old tired voice. "You have both seen the man, Peters. What conclusions have you drawn?"

"Dope," said Jeff quietly.

"I agree," said the old doctor. "Though horribly emaciated, he bears no trace of disease."

"Exactly." The man at the lead of the table nodded, and glanced down at some papers spread before him. "You may be surprised to hear that Peters is not the only case of its kind we have discovered. Lately several people have been found in similar condition—wealthy people, some young, the majority old." He leaned back in his chair. "Obviously their condition was caused by dope. The question is—which dope?"

"Peters came from Venus," Jeff said slowly. "He could have contracted the habit there."

"Probably, and yet he showed absolutely no signs of addiction on arrival. The reasons for his resignation were 'Personal and Private.' An officer of his standing is not required to give further information, but I have it on good authority that he had become embroiled in trouble with the natives."

"On Venus?" Jeff glanced at the doctor beside him, then towards the head of the table. "I hadn't known about that."

"There was no reason why you should. The military have kept it very quiet."

"Could the Venusians have inoculated him with the drug?"

"Probably, but we are getting away from the main point." Deliberately the man with the tired-face and the old voice tapped the papers before him. "Peters is not an isolated case. There have been others, which points, I think, to clear evidence of some new exotic drug. Our problem is a simple one—we must find just which drug it is, and just how it arrives here."

"Peters showed traces of surgery," said the old doctor. "It is conceivable that he could have had a container of the drug imbedded in the muscles of his back. If the container were thin and organic, it wouldn't have shown on the X-ray screens at Tycho."

"Admitted. Yet we mustn't forget just what kind of a man Peters was. Is it conceivable that a man such as Peters, the commander of the Venusian garrison, would have consented to smuggle drugs? And for what? He threw away everything he'd worked for, resigned his commission, returned to Earth—and rotted in a gutter." Slowly the man shook his head.

"We have a mystery here, gentlemen. And mysteries must be solved."

"The other cases," said Jeff suddenly. "Are they confined to the elite?"

"Yes. Mostly leaders of society, statesmen, high ranking officers and diplomats." The man at the head of the table sighed a little. "That is what makes our task both difficult and important. Naturally we could get no admissions from those directly concerned."

"It would seem that the origin of this mysterious drug is on Venus," Jeff said quietly "Am I to go there?"

"Yes. You will travel on the midnight rocket, and a usual you will have a free hand." He rose and Jeff rose with him.

"You know what you must do. Find the drug, find the men responsible for distributing it, and smash them utterly."

He nodded in dismissal, and Jeff turned, waiting for the release of the electronic lock holding the door.

He felt strangely alone.

* * * *

Heat and wilting humidity, a lowering blanket of sullen cloud blotched with the golden radiance of a hidden sun. Tremendous fern trees springing from rich black loam, their great leaves casting a dim, mist-like shadow, giving a false impression of coolness.

Venus!

A place of mystery, a hothouse world, rich, bursting with minerals and medicinal plants. A place of eternal rain and damp, a planet of heat and strength-sapping climate, a world of promise to land-starved Earthmen.

Jeff stood at the foot of the loading ramp, the towering grace of the rocket ship soaring behind him, the flame-seared dirt of the landing field harsh and gritty beneath his feet. He waited there, staring at the twenty foot high, wire-mesh fence surrounding the field, the huddle of crude shanties hugging the outer perimeter, and the spotted metal of the administration buildings.

It was just the same.

The same mixture of the ultra-modern and the primitive. Rocket ships of gleaming alloy, and shanties of branches and interlaced leaves. The fence, bright and wonderful with the magic of trapped droplets of moisture, and against that beauty the squalor of men too busy making money to remember how to live.

Even the drums were the same.

The throb and pulse of the eternal drums. The half-heard yet always-felt cadence of beaten skin, disturbed membrane, agitated diaphragms. Even the leaves of the great trees added to the planetary rhythm, whispering as swollen droplets of rain splashed from one to the other.

Drums!

Jeff shrugged, trying not to feel the discomfort of his sodden flesh as his thin clothing clung damply to him. He turned his head as a man strode across the field towards him, and picking up his minimum kit, went to meet him.

"Walker?"

"Yes."

"I'm Carmody, commander here. They told me you were coming."

Jeff nodded, and fell into step beside the commander. Like Peters he was a military man, a professional soldier, tall and rigid, his uniform clean and his insignia bright and shining. He strode briskly across the seared dirt of the field, not saying anything, not even looking at his visitor, a man too conscious of his own importance for the smaller things of life, the gentler things such as consideration for others. He didn't speak until they had entered the office in the fungi-spotted administration building.

"Earth radioed that you were coming. They asked me to assist you in every way possible, and place myself your disposal." He sounded curt and very disinterested.

"As commander here think I should be informed to the reason for your visit."

"Naturally," said Jeff mildly. He looked around the office, dropping his kit and relaxing into a chair. He smiled at the grim face of the commander, and fumbled his pocket for a cigarette. The package was a sodden ruin, the tobacco bursting from the thin paper wrappings, and he stared at them with dismay.

"Here." Carmody threw a package towards Jeff. "Untreated cigarettes are useless here. These have a silicon film, to make them waterproof."

"Thanks." Jeff took one and carefully lit it, inhaling gratefully at the blue smoke. "I'd forgotten."

He hadn't forgotten. No one who had ever been to Venus could ever forget the eternal damp, but the incident had served to break the ice.

"I'm from Exotic," he said abruptly. "Earth couldn't radio you what all this is about because as yet it's pretty secret. Naturally I'm here to brief you as well as to ask your assistance."

"That isn't what they told me," snapped the commander. "The way I heard it was that you're to take over everything but my uniform."

"No." Jeff smiled again and dragged at his cigarette. "I'm not interested in giving orders. I wouldn't even know how, and obviously you are the one man who would be able to help me most."

He stared at the softening lines of the commander's features, and tried not to grin. It always worked! A terse command from Earth, the natural irritation of a man with an overdose of personal pride and inflated dignity, and then the smoothing down. Carmody would feel grateful to Jeff for not sticking to the letter of the original order, and would be more inclined to help. If he didn't? Jeff smiled behind the thin haze of blue smoke. He still had the original instructions to fall back on.

"What is it you want to know?"

"What happened to Peters?"

"What?"

Carmody's surprise was genuine. He stared at Jeff as if he doubted what he had heard, his little eyes narrowing against the pallor of his face.

"Peters," said Jeff patiently. "The man who was in command before you. You must know him."

"I know him, yes, but you didn't ask that."

"I asked what happened to him?"

"He resigned, and went back to Earth. Why?"

"That's what I want to know."

"I meant, why do you ask?"

Jeff didn't reply. He stared at the smouldering end of his cigarette for a moment, then crushed it beneath his heel.

"Look," he said quietly. "I'd appreciate it if you would get one thing straight. I ask the questions. Now I'm not interested in any code of loyalty you may have, and if you think that you're helping Peters by acting dumb, forget it. This thing is bigger than any one man."

Carmody reddened, his sallow features stiffening with affronted dignity and injured self-conceit, his small eyes glittering with anger.

"You…" he said. "You…"

"Hold it," Jeff warned. "I intended no personal insult, but you haven't seen Peters lately. I have."

"You've seen him? On Earth?"

"Yes."

"I see." Carmody slumped in his chair, his eyes dull and his anger vanishing as he stared at the calm features of the man before him. "Did he…" He paused, running the tip of his tongue over his lips. "Did he say anything?"

"I ask the questions," reminded Jeff quietly. He stared at the commander. "You were here when Peters was commander, you took over from him when he left. I want to know what made him leave."

"I don't know."

Jeff shrugged, not saying anything, just sitting and staring at the commander. Carmody shifted in his chair and nervously reached for a cigarette.

"He didn't tell me why he resigned," he blurted desperately. "I'm not holding anything back. Peters was a secretive man, and didn't encourage social contacts with his under officers. There were rumours of course, but in a place like this there are always rumours."

"Such as?"

"The usual thing. Women, drink. Some hinted that he took too great an interest in the natives, a dozen things."

"Did he have any friends here? Close friends I mean?"

"There was one man, a captain; they seemed pretty close."

"Could I see this man?"

"No."

"Why not?"

"He died three months ago," said Carmody quietly, and Jeff could sense the man's triumph in his small victory.

"How?

The commander shrugged. "A fight I think. He was found at the edge of the wire with a knife in his back, a native weapon. We took punitive measures of course."

"Naturally," said Jeff dryly, "but it doesn't need a native to use a knife, or hadn't you thought of that?"

"I'm not quite the fool you seem to think, Walker. I investigated, but we'd been having trouble with the natives for some time and it was obvious that they were to blame."

"Trouble?"

"Yes. Open cast mining of mineral ores was started six months ago. The natives objected and we had to subdue them."

"I see." Jeff reached for a cigarette and frowned through the veil of blue smoke. "I didn't know that. Why wasn't it reported?"

"It was. First by Peters, then by myself in our routine reports." He shrugged and gestured, with his hand. "It was a small matter; we handled it with ease. No need to make it bigger than it actually was." He stared at Jeff. "What has all this to do with your mission here? And incidentally, you haven't told me yet what it is."

"No," agreed Jeff. "I haven't." He leaned forward in his chair, staring at the cultivated sternness of the commander's face. "Someone has been smuggling drugs from Venus to Earth, narcotic drugs of a particularly unpleasant nature. I am here to stop it."

Carmody laughed.

He leaned back in his chair, his mouth open, his small eyes squeezed shut, and the sound of his laughter sent little ripples of irritation racing up Jeff's spine. He waited until the commander had regained self-control, then continued as if there had been no interruption.

"Peters was an addict, and Peters was also a carrier. Does that amuse you, too?"

"What! Peters an addict? I don't believe it!"

"You would believe it if you could see him," said Jeff grimly. "Imagine Peters as you knew him, and then imagine the lowest form of human life possible. That is what Peters has become, dirty, verminous, stinking and rotten. If he lives he'll be lucky; if he regains his sanity it will be a miracle. Do you still feel like laughing?"

"But smuggling drugs from Venus! It's impossible!"

"Why?"

"We search every passenger, every ship, every cargo. They are searched again on Tycho, and again on Earth. How could contraband get through?"

"It does, but that isn't your concern. Your worry is to help me find out who is doing it."

Jeff rose from the chair and, crossing the office, stared out of the speckled windows. Below him the landing field showed as a raw, seared patch against the yellow-green of the jungle, the high wire fence as a subdued cobweb spun by some enormous spider. The delicate spires of rocket ships glistened with rain as they waited for their loads of processed goods, their ports open, their loading ramps down.

He frowned as a long file of men entered the compound. They carried rifles, the long-barrelled, high-velocity weapons of the garrison, and their faces showed pale and haggard as they marched across the field towards their quarters.

"I see that your soldiers have been on duty," he said.

"Trouble?"

"I told you, the natives had to be subdued when we started open cast mining." Carmody joined Jeff at the window. "Those men have been on guard. We have too much expensive equipment lying about the site for comfort and the operators are touchy about it."

"That must keep you pretty busy," mused Jeff. "What with servicing the rockets, guarding the landing field and settlement, now the mining sites, how do you manage for men?"

"We do our best," said Carmody stiffly. He sighed and wiped his face and neck with a square of damp linen. "We just haven't enough men," he confessed. "If this were a totally military operation it wouldn't matter, but it's not. The garrison is expected to protect every man and piece of property on the planet, and it's getting to the point where we just can't do it. The operators are only concerned with getting as much as they can while they can. Every spare man is snapped up. I've even known offers made to my soldiers persuading them to desert and work for one of the companies. And what with the trouble with the natives and the pressure from back home…"
He bit his lips and let the words die into silence.

"Why can't the operators guard their own property?"

"They are too busy working, and employees are expensive. The military serve as cheap labour."

Jeff was surprised at the bitterness in the commander's voice. He nodded, then opened the window, hoping for a breeze from the wire mesh screen. There was no breeze, and he leaned close to the corroded metal, gulping great breaths of the humid air. As usual the drums were beating, and automatically his heart began to adjust to the throb and pulse of the murmuring rhythm. Beside him Carmody snarled a curse.

"Those blasted drums! I'd like to smash every one of them!"

"Are they always as bad as this?"

"Lately they've hardly ever stopped. Ever since the trouble six months ago I've had to listen to them and I'm just about getting sick of it." He snorted and slammed shut the window. "What about you, Walker? Are you going to stay here?"

"No. Officially you know nothing about me. I'll go into the settlement, drift around, see what I can pick up. I'll contact you if I need anything, and in the meantime try and remember everything you ever knew about Peters." He grinned at the commander's relieved expression and picked up his kit. Outside it was darker. It looked as though a storm was coming.

* * * *

The settlement was filthy. It was dirty with the accumulated refuse of men too busy to tidy up, too lazy to keep their shacks clean, too indolent to perform the essentials of civilised life.

Heaps of empty containers reared their ugly bulk between the great boles of the fern trees. Scraps of waxed paper, shreds of clothing, discarded rinds of fruits, rotting fragments of food and other garbage. A smell hung over the huddle of crude shelters, the stench of cesspools and poor sanitation, the reek of dirt and decay.

It was the product of civilised men too busy to tidy up, too eager to rape a new world of its wealth and without the time or inclination to bury their own filth. It was an environment where alcohol provided an easy euphoria—and where, drugs would find a ready market.

Jeff hesitated in the centre of the huddle, his nostrils wrinkling as the humid air transmitted the unmistakable odour of sewage. He hefted the minimum kit in his hand, then strode across the central clearing, his feet squelching in the semi-liquid ooze between the shacks.

Noise spilled from one of the largest of the shacks, a steady drone of conversation, the welcome sound of clicking glasses and the discordant shrill of mechanically reproduced music. He recognised the place—it was the trading post, drinking centre, hub of what communal life existed on the planet. Shrugging, he entered the sprawling shelter. Men stared at him as he thrust past them. Pale men with bleached features and soggy skins. They wore loincloths and sandals and most of them had weapons belted around their waists. Knives, high-velocity pistols, even a few short range flare-guns capable of incinerating an animal the size of a large dog with their blast of energy. They stared at him, half-curious, half-indifferent, and he paid them the same attention.

The trader was a fat man with a bulging paunch and hairy chest. He nodded at Jeff, setting a bottle and glass on the counter and squinting at the coins Jeff tossed on the rough wooden planking.

"New here, aren't you?"

"Just arrived." Jeff tilted the bottle, half-filling the thick glass with the locally distilled spirit. "Know where I can find an empty shack?"

"You working?"

"Not yet." Jeff smiled as he sipped at the crude liquor. "I told you, I've just arrived."

"If you want a job I can fix you up," suggested the fat man. "Plenty of work out at the new site, or maybe you'd like to work here with me." He looked hopefully at the young man. "Good food, plenty of liquor and I'll cut you in to a share of the profits."

"Thanks." Jeff shrugged and stared at the crowded bar. "I'll think about it, but now I need a shack."

"Take your pick." The fat man waved a dirty hand towards the huddle of shelters. "Most of the boys have moved out to the open cast mining site. They took over a village there, so you're bound to find an empty shack close to the wire."

"I'll do that," said Jeff. "Thanks."

He rested his back against the bar, hooking his elbows on the edge of the counter, and stared at the men clustered in the trading post. They were all the same. All had the same expression, the same look of hungry greed, the same nerve-twitching impatience to make their pile and get back home. They drank with a quiet desperation, the sound of their conversation a steady hum, and the talk of each one was a carbon-copy of the others'.

Money!

They thought of nothing else, talked of nothing else; they lived and breathed it, counted it a thousand times in their dreams and schemed a thousand ways in their few leisure moments. Venus was rich! Venus was a world without labour and with products worth their weight in refined uranium back on Earth.

"I'm getting out as soon as my indenture's finished," said one man to another. "The company aren't going to keep me slaving for a wage when I can pick up a fortune on one trip. Twenty kilo of those rejuvenating spores and I can retire a rich man."

"Why wait?" His listener drained his glass and rapped on the counter. "Why not just walk out and forget your indenture?"

"I hear that the natives are thinking of working for us," said a third. "About time those damn Venis did some work. Why should we sweat while they sit on their rears?"

"I know what I'd like to do," said the first man. "I'd like to round them up from one of their villages and put 'em all to work gathering medicinal plants." He winked. "Naturally they'd turn the plants over to me, and naturally I'd pay for them."

"How much would you pay, Sam?" The fat trader hung his paunch over the edge of the counter as he joined the conversation. "I've a load of trade goods I can't get rid of, beads and junk like that. Those natives ought to be glad to take them."

"Don't need them," said Sam cheerfully. "All I want is a worm so I can make my own liquor. I'd pay 'em off in booze, and once they'd got the craving I'd work 'em to death for a pint a day."

"You've got an idea there, Sam," said the second man excitedly. "What say we try it out?"

"What about the military?" The fat trader stared at the flushed faces of his half-drunken listeners. "Don't forget they're supposed to keep order here."

"That only applies to us," said Sam. "Anyway those soldier boys are so poor that we could buy them off at our own price." He grinned and nudged his companion. "Don't forget they're human just like the rest of us, and if they don't make their pile now they never will."

The mechanical juke box suddenly whined into silence, and in the hush the pulsing sound of the murmuring drums seemed loud.

"Start that thing up again," yelled Sam, his mouth twisted into ugly lines. "Kill those damn drums! They're driving me crazy."

"We gotta do something about that," snarled a scar-faced man. "We oughta make Carmody do something. How can a man work while that racket pounds in his ears?"

A low mutter of agreement rumbled across the men, and Jeff moved from the bar trying not to show his emotions.

He felt sick!

He felt ashamed of being a man, of being a member of the same race as the men who were despoiling a planet. He thrust between the crowd of near-naked workers and stood for a moment gulping at the heavy air in the clearing.

Thunder muttered low on the horizon, and a ghost of a breeze stirred the wide leaves of the fern trees. Light flared briefly as jagged fingers of lightning thrust across the sullen clouds, and hastily he squelched through the mire towards the empty shelters close to the wire.

He found a sagging wreck which might help to keep off some of the rain. He kicked the worst refuse into the alley before the open front of the shelter, then slumped down on the leaf-covered bed, and stared at the interlaced leaves of the low roof.

Thinking.

He felt very tired and his muscles ached from unaccustomed exercise after the long weeks of free fall, but worse than that was his reaction to what he had seen and heard.

He frowned, trying to remember whether or not it had been the same on his last visit, then decided that it hadn't. The tempo had quickened. The fever had taken over—get rich quick and to hell with the consequences. There was a different atmosphere, an uglier one, one which was rapidly nearing a critical pitch of violent action.

He didn't like it.

It wasn't so much what they had said; men had always talked wildly, spinning dreams from the tenuous threads of imagination. It was how they had said it. They were serious, they really meant what they said, and from idle talk over a drink in a bar to sudden ugly action was sometimes too short a step.

He shifted uneasily on the hard bed of leaves and woven branches, then reached into his kit for a package of silicon-filmed cigarettes. He inhaled deeply, letting the fragrant smoke stream from his nostrils, and let his thoughts scurry like a trapped rat's within the confines of his skull.

Outside, the clouds had grown darker, the mutter of distant thunder more regular, merging with the half-heard pulse of the drums.

The drums!

He sat up on the crude bed and narrowed his eyes in startled thought. Drums were natural on Venus, a part of the native life, as much a part as the whining radios were a part of Terrestrial civilisation, but never had he known them pound with such monotonous regularity.

To the natives they were a religion, an integral part of their way of life. He had seen one of their ceremonies, the people sitting in a circle around the drummer, swaying to the rhythm, swaying for hours, their eyes closed, their every sense dulled by the cadence. He knew the theory behind such ritual, the scientific fact that the beat of the heart tends to align itself to the pulse of the drum. More than that he didn't know, but the natives...?

He shook his head. The last thing they could want would be to arouse the Earthmen to hysterical rage. No, the drums must have another explanation.

He grunted, tugging off his wet shirt and trousers, strapping his weapon belt around the tops of his shorts. The humidity had grown worse and his flesh felt clammy as his own perspiration struggled to evaporate into an atmosphere already overloaded with moisture. The tension in the air made his nerves twitch so that it seemed as if many-legged insects were running over his skin, and he brushed at them before he realised they were a product of his imagination.

Feet squelched close to his shack, two pairs of feet, and with them came the mutter of low voices.

"You sure he's coming this way?"

"Yeah. Ready?"

The first speaker chuckled.

"Get under cover. I'll handle him and make sure that the other one doesn't get away. Hurry now!"

Jeff tensed, then silently moved towards the front of the shack. He hesitated, undecided whether or not to walk out and betray his presence, or stay where was. Life on the frontiers was harsh and sometimes it paid a man to mind his own business.

Equally so, violence was everyone's business.

He paused by the open front of the shack, squinting through the fine mist, trying to make out the speakers. A shadow drifted between the shacks, a tall graceful shadow, and watching it, Jeff crouched down behind the flimsy shelter of the woven branches, his eyes narrowed in thought.

The man was a native.

He strode lithely over the muck, his dead-white skin almost luminous in the mist, his snow-white hair falling like gossamer to his shoulders. He was naked but for a loin cloth and sandals, weaponless, and yet he moved with a quiet assurance as if he were among friends instead of men who despised and hated every member of his race.

The trouble was he looked too much like a man.

An animal would have been accepted. A savage, something alien and horrible—that was expected, but the natives weren't like that. They were tall, humanoid, albino—and they regarded Earthmen with a quiet and deadly contempt.

Jeff watched him as he strode over the clearing, his white skin shining and clean, his hair spotless. He watched him, and compared him to the men who were busy ravaging his planet, the big, sweating men, the money-hungry crowd, the smart boys and the work-shy.

It made him feel ashamed.

From somewhere beside him, on the other side of the flimsy wall, he heard the hiss of indrawn breath. Thunder snarled overhead, thunder and the eye-searing flash of lightning. The thunder crashed again—and with it merged another sound.

The spiteful crack of a high-velocity pistol! And with the sound came the hissing thunder of the rain.

* * * *

Rain!

It filled the heavy air with mist, spattering on the mud and drumming on the wide leaves of the fern trees. It choked and clogged, making it almost impossible to breathe and drenching everything inside shelter or out. Mingled with the rain came the thunder and lightning, great peals of stupendous noise and stabbing shafts of brilliance. It filled the universe with elemental fury, raging and blasting with blind torrents of energy.

Jeff crouched by the wall of his hut, his eyes filled with water, his body soaked with it, struggling to breathe without drowning, cringing as he waited for the storm to pass.

As swiftly as it had come, the rain died, the thunder muted, the stabbing shafts of lightning passed on. The storm centre moved past the settlement, and aside from the heavy mist and streaming fern trees, things were as before.

Almost.

Jeff stared at the crumpled figure lying in the mud, the long white hair caked with dirt, the pale skin soiled and blotched with the twin combinations of mud and blood.

He stared at the figure, then slowly reached for his own weapon and took one stride towards the open front of his hut. One stride, then stopped at the sound of voices. "O.K., Fred?"

"Yeah. Got him just right. I hope the rain didn't drown him."

"Nah." The second voice held utter contempt. "Those things don't drown. You think the other one will be here soon?"

"Sure to be; never known it fail yet. Keep quiet now." Jeff bit his lips, staring at the feebly twitching figure of the native. Every instinct within him screamed for him to go to the man's aid, and yet the cold certainty that if he did would earn him swift death, forced him to remain where he was.

He glanced about the hut. Apart from the open front, there was no way out, no way that he could escape without making noise, and that would mean the nerve shocking bite of high-velocity slugs. He could do nothing but wait, and so he waited, his hand tight around the butt of his gun.

He didn't have to wait long. A second shadow moved between the huts, a second native, tall, proud, weaponless, and yet different from the first.

He bore markings on his white flesh, an intricate pattern of black, a subtle interweaving of jet, so that he appeared to be a walking harmony of night and day. A fillet of beaten metal holding a stone of peculiar brilliance contained his hair, the stone centred in the middle of his forehead. He carried a gourd at his waist and he appeared to be very old. Jeff had never seen a native like him before.

He paused as he saw the crumpled figure in the mud, paused, and stared about him as if looking for something or someone. For a long moment he stood there, tall and calm and radiating a simple dignity, then he moved—and Jeff moved with him.

He sprang, his legs thrusting at the dirt, his eyes darting as he scanned the area, and the pistol in his hand jerking to swift aim. A man stared at him from beside the hut, a pale-faced man with a pistol in his hand. Jeff shot him, then flung himself to the mud as a gun flamed at him from the shelter of a tree.

He wriggled, squirming desperately as he tried to dodge bullets and take aim at the same time. Again the hidden man fired, again, the tiny slugs sending little geysers of mud and water spouting into the air. Jeff fired, swore as his bullet exploded into incandescent vapour against the bole of the tree, then fired again at a flash of white.

The man screamed, jerking from behind the tree, his hand a red ruin and his face a terrified mask. He stared at Jeff, stared at the menacing orifice of the weapon, then ran desperately among the shielding trees, blood dripping from his hand and leaving a red trail over the watery mud.

Jeff watched him go, then climbed slowly to his feet. The strangely marked native still stood by the side of the crumpled man, still calm, still seemingly unperturbed by what had happened, but his eyes as they stared at Jeff were filled with hidden thoughts.

Jeff ignored him. He knelt by the side of the injured man, and gently examined the ugly wound in the white flesh.

"Help me," he snapped. "We must take him to the hospital. Unless he gets attention he will die."

The native didn't move.

"Quickly," snapped Jeff impatiently, then realising that perhaps the man knew no English, made gestures in pantomime.

Still the man made no move.

"Blast you," snorted Jeff angrily. "If you won't help me I'll carry him myself."

"No."

"What?" Jeff paused as he stared at the tall figure. "So you can speak English. Hurry now, help me get your friend to hospital."

"No."

"Why not? We may be able to save him."

The injured man groaned, stirring a little in the mud, and staring at Jeff with pain-filled eyes. He saw the oddly marked native, and smiled, his eyes brightening with something like hope.

"Your science could not save him," said the tall native with quiet certainty. He stooped over the white body, thrusting himself between Jeff and the injured man. One hand went to the gourd at his waist, the other supporting the dirt-caked head. He said something, his voice a low murmur, then his hand touched the injured man's lips, and he straightened, staring down at the dying man.

Jeff stared with him, and together they watched him die.

It was a peaceful passing. All pain had gone, all discomfort; it was as if the man had fallen asleep and while still asleep had passed into the great dark. Jeff sighed a little, then reluctantly examined the body of the man he had shot. He was quite dead, his head exploded into internal ruin by the high-velocity bullet, and Jeff looked down at him with a puzzled frown.

"Why did he kill your friend?"

"He did not kill, only wound," reminded the oddly marked native. He glanced at the body in the mud before them. "Why did you kill your friend?"

"He wasn't my friend," said Jeff savagely. "Believe it or not we aren't all the same, and we have our own methods of dealing with those who forget what they should be."

"Yet we are as nothing to you. Would you kill one of your own for nothing?" There was a cynical halftone to the quiet voice and Jeff glanced sharply at the native. "You speak remarkably good English," he said. "How did you learn it?"

"When first men landed here in their ships of fire, they did not then consider us as less than dirt. We welcomed them, for they sought knowledge, and in return they told us those things they considered necessary for us to know. Your language was one such thing. There were others, many others. Of them all, perhaps the language is the most important."

"You think so?" Jeff looked his surprise. "Important, yes, but surely there are other things, the use of metal, medicine, hygiene, a thousand advantages must be gained from contact with a civilisation with a higher technology?"

"Perhaps, and yet we consider your language to be most revealing." The tall native glanced down at the silent body of the Venusian. "My work is done here. I must go, and yet there is something still to do."

"Yes?"

"The man with the injured hand, you know him?"

"No, but I can find him," said Jeff grimly. "He'll be bound to go to the hospital for treatment, and when he does I'll be waiting for him."

"Why?"

"Why?" Jeff stared at the tall man and shook his head. "What's the matter with you? That man and his friend deliberately shot a native. They didn't even kill him, just left him there in the mud and wet while they waited to kill you too. Isn't that reason enough for punishment?"

"Will this punishment restore life to the dead?"

"No, but it will safeguard the living."

"Perhaps, and yet again perhaps not. I think it would be as well to forget your desire for inflicting punishment."

"Think what you like," snapped Jeff curtly. "You have nothing to do with it."

"It is we that will suffer," said the tall man quietly. "Have you thought of that?"

"You suffer?" Jeff laughed without humour, trying not to show his impatience. "What's the matter with you? Can't you even think straight any more? What has my dealing with a potential killer to do with you? That man is dangerous; he can't be allowed to get away with what he's done, and I'm going to see that he doesn't."

"What has he done?" The tall man lowered his pink, albino eyes as he stared at the tranquil features of the dead native. "He has helped to kill a Venusian. What does that mean to your people? Would the commander of your garrison worry about such a trifle when he himself is responsible for the deaths of over three hundred of us, responsible for the occupying of four of our villages and the destruction of ten square miles of forest? Would the fact that he shot a native count against the fact that Earthmen are scarce here and that every man is needed for exploiting the new mining site?"

"That has nothing to do with it," snapped Jeff. "This is personal. I can't worry about intangibles, I can only worry about what has happened, and what may happen again."

"One man has died," reminded the tall native gently. "A life for a life. Isn't that what you teach?"

"I don't understand," said Jeff slowly. "I can't follow your logic. Do you want to be driven into the dirt? I'm not against my own race, but I'm against a certain element of it, and that element must be stamped out. I'm not even concerned with what happens to your people. The strong must take care of themselves, and if they are weak and not strong, then they must yield. That is a law of life, jungle law if you like, but still a law."

"Your law," said the native, "not ours."

"Maybe, but we live by our law, not yours."

He looked at the native, at the fine proud features, the wide intelligent eyes, and the body that was so much like a human body. He felt a strange affinity for the Venusian, a strange longing to be respected by him, respected and liked.

"You know," he said slowly. "Something wrong has happened between our peoples. Here we are, you and I, talking as any two intelligent men can talk. Why can't it always be like this? Why has this difference arisen? Why do you make us feel ashamed so that in reaction we treat you as if you were animals?"

"You know the answer," reminded the native quietly. He stood for a moment looking down at the dead Venusian, then without a word, without a second glance, he had gone, swallowed up in the mist and the dimness between the great trees. Jeff stared after him, and the truth of what he had said was bitter in his mouth.

He did know.

Men had come to Venus on the wings of high adventure, and those men had been good. Others had followed them, the hard-headed business men, the exploiters, the self-seekers and the get-rich-quick fraternity. Venus was rich. Venus was ripe for the plucking. Venus had intelligent life, natives who could work the plantations and mines—but the natives wouldn't play!

They hadn't wanted the trade goods, the cheap trash, the petty, glittering things designed to catch the eye and wear out in a predictable time. They hadn't even wanted money to buy artifacts from Earth. They had wanted nothing, not even contact, and so men had nursed their resentment and counted the money they could have earned—if!

If the natives had agreed to work. If the Venusians had agreed to sweat for goods they couldn't use, clothes they didn't want, luxuries they were better without. Men had come bearing gifts—and those gifts had been scorned. They had brought the one unfailing weapon—and' it had crumbled in their hand. For once in the history of man he hadn't been able to buy what he wanted, and the discovery made him realise just how much his money was worth.

The discovery had filled him with hate.

And so had come the garrison, the armed soldiers, the stern-faced military. They took what they wanted, took more than they could use, and like a rotten cancer the settlement spilled its filth into the once-fair forests. Men grew careless, wasteful, wantonly destructive. Why not? They had a whole new planet to play with. What did it matter if a few extra trees were cut, some top soil destroyed, food sources ruined? Hell, there was plenty more wasn't there?

Jeff shrugged and wished he were back home. Back where things were familiar, where a man didn't have to talk with a tall, quiet-eyed savage with a too-keen brain. Where money had its correct worth and men didn't kill without reason.

Slowly he began to follow the almost washed-out blood trail, moving with his eyes to the ground, his body stooped and relaxed.

He didn't want to think about it.

* * * *

The blood trail led directly to the hospital, a prefabricated structure of metal and plastic, spotted with fungi and streaming with condensed moisture. Jeff thrust past the guard at the gate of the high wire fence, slammed open the double doors, and glared at the white-faced man sitting on a bench, his hand wrapped in crude bandages.

"All right, you," he snapped. "Come with me."

"Where to?"

"To the commander. I'm accusing you of attempted murder."

A doctor, his thin white smock stained and mottled with damp and chemicals, entered the room and glanced at Jeff.

"What's all this about?"

"I'm taking this man to Carmody," said Jeff tightly. "He tried to kill me. If I hadn't shot the gun from his hand he would have succeeded."

"That's a lie," snarled the man. He looked at the doctor. "I was with a friend of mine. We'd gone to the old shacks for shelter during the storm. This man shot Fred and would have killed me if I hadn't been lucky." He winced as he stared at his bandaged hand. "Fix me up, will you, doc? This hand is giving me hell!"

The doctor grunted, deftly cutting away the crude bandages and pursing his lips as he saw the nature of the wound.

"How is it, doc?"

"Not too bad. You won't lose the hand—just a couple of fingers." He reached for a jar of alcohol and began to swab away the caked blood and dirt. Jeff hesitated, looking at the pain-distorted features of the injured man.

"What's your name?"

"Gill Murphy," said the doctor quietly before the man could answer. "Now will you get out of here? I don't like an audience when I operate."

"Is that your name, doc, or his?"

"His."

"Thanks." Jeff turned and slammed angrily from the hospital. A guard stared at him with dull, incurious eyes as he headed for the administration building, and a young under officer stopped him just within the door.

"Yes?"

"I want to see Carmody," snapped Jeff. "Is he here?"

"Who are you? What is your business? Have you an appointment?"

"Jeff Walker. Private. No. Does all that satisfy you or do you still want to play games?" Jeff glared at the young man. "Tell Carmody I'm here; he'll see me—and don't take all day doing it."

"If you will take a seat," said the young officer stiffly, "I will see whether the commander is free."

He marched away, a young man with dead white skin and short-cropped hair, uncomfortable in the prison of his thin uniform, yet needing it to bolster his pride. Jeff stared after him, then dropped into a chair, fumbling in his belt sack for cigarettes. He lit one, dragging the smoke deep into his lungs, and stared out of the open door towards the dull glimmer of the surrounding fence.

Five cigarettes later he was still waiting.

Five cigarettes, thirty minutes, time for murder, for intrigue, for escape. Time to do a dozen things, hide a dozen people, burn papers, walk a couple of miles. Time, too much time. Carmody couldn't have been that busy.

He lunged to his feet as the young officer returned, crushing the smouldering butt of his cigarette beneath his san dal, and striding impatiently forward.

"Well?"

"The commander will see you," said the young man regretfully. "Follow me please."

Still armoured in the dignity of his uncomfortable uniform, he led the way to Carmody.

The commander sat in his chair behind the wide expanse of his desk. Behind him the windows were open; even the wire mesh screens had been swung aside. An electric fan whispered softly as its blade sliced through the thick air, and the room was redolent with the scent of burning tobacco.

Jeff paused just within the door, closing it carefully behind him, and his nostril flared a little as a familiar odour triggered dormant memory. He said nothing, just sat and looked at the tense features of the commander, waiting for him to speak.

"You wanted to see me?"

"Yes. Why did I have to wait so long?"

"Really, Walker!" Carmody gestured at the papers littering his desk. "I was busy and the young fool who brought your message forgot your name. I'm sorry, but there it is." He dabbed at his face and neck with a sodden handkerchief. "What can I do for you?"

"Arrest a man named Gill Murphy. He was in the hospital having treatment for an injured hand. I want you to pull him in and charge him with attempted murder."

"Murder?"

"Yes, my murder." Jeff reached for a cigarette and stared at Carmody through a haze of blue smoke. "There were two of them; I don't know the other man's name, and they were waiting to kill a couple of natives. They shot one; he died later. I interfered before they could finish the job—killed one and wounded Murphy." He dragged at the smouldering cigarette.

"I left him down in the hospital. My bullet smashed his hand. The doc said that he would lose a couple of fingers, so you shouldn't have trouble picking him up."

"I see." Carmody moved some of the papers on the desk and avoided looking at Jeff. "You killed a man, an Earthman?"

"Yes."

"Why?"

"Why?" Jeff stared his surprise. "I told you—they were lying in wait for the natives. Damn it, man, did you want me to watch murder?"

"Murder?" Carmody shook his head. "Natives aren't men, Walker. You can't murder an animal. You did wrong to kill that Earthman; you shouldn't have interfered." He frowned down at the papers on his desk and nodded with sudden decision. "I think you had better catch the next rocket back to Earth. As commander here I feel it my duty to order your return."

"What!"

"Yes. You've killed an Earthman, wounded another. They don't know what you are or why you are here, and even if they did they wouldn't have any sympathy for a snoop. Your life isn't worth a light once they learn of it, and Murphy isn't the sort of man to keep his mouth shut."

He nodded again, his thin mouth a tight gash across the pallor of his stern features.

"It is my duty to safeguard you, Walker. You will return on the next ship."

"Like hell I will!" Jeff stared at the man, his eyes narrowed and anger sending a dull flush of colour over his dying tan. "I came here to do a job, Carmody, and I'm not leaving until it's done."

"You should have thought of that before," said the commander tersely. "A dead man can't do jobs, and believe me, Walker, once you leave this area you are as good as dead."

"Am I?" said Jeff softly. He slumped in the chair forcing his muscles to relax fighting the anger burning inside him. He reached for a cigarette.

"Tell me, Carmody, why should men want to kil natives?"

"How do I know?" The commander shrugged and leaned back in his chair. "Maybe they didn't like the idea of the natives prowling through the settlement. Perhaps the drums had got on their nerves and it was their way of releasing tension Maybe it was just one of those things. Why do men kill, anyway?"

"Usually for a very good reason." Jeff stared at the smouldering tip of his cigarette. "They knew what they were doing, those men. This was no revenge killing, no sudden impulse or outbreak of nerves. They deliberately wounded one and then lay waiting for the other. They knew that he would be along, knew it!" He looked at the tense face of the man behind the desk.

"How would they know a thing like that, Carmody?"

"I don't know."

"There was reason behind it all," mused Jeff. "Cold, logical reason. You know what those men reminded me of? They reminded me of hunters, setting a snare for valuable game. They didn't want the first man; he merely served as bait. They wanted the other one, and it was necessary to wound the first native almost to death in order to get him."

"Ridiculous!"

"Is it, Carmody? Perhaps you're right, I wouldn't know. Tell me, how long have you been on Venus?"

"Several years now. Why?"

"You must have learned quite a bit about the natives in that time—their customs, their ritual, the way they live and think. Do you know why some of the natives wear black markings? An intricate pattern of jet tattooed into the skin?"

"Yes."

The commander shifted uncomfortably in his chair. "You mean the Shamans, the medicine men. They are similar to our own African witch doctors."

"Is *that* what they are?" Jeff leaned back and closed his eyes. The heat sapped at his strength and the ghastly humidity wrapped him in warm, wet cotton wool. His mouth felt sore from too much smoking and his nerves twitched and jumped in irritation.

Carmody stared at him, then reached into an open drawer. "You looked pooped. Want a drink?"

"Thanks." Jeff opened his eyes and watched the commander pour two glasses half-full of watery liquid. "Maybe you're right, Carmody. Maybe I'm wasting my time here. The drugs must be coming from some other place, and yet…" He smiled and reached for the glass. "How did Peters get the way he was?"

"Who knows?" Carmody sipped at the alcohol and licked his lips. "We get all kinds stop off here—ships from Mars and Mercury. He could have got the stuff from one of them, and maybe the drums decided him to resign." He stared out of the window, the sweat shining on his flabby cheeks. "It wouldn't take much to make a man decide to quit. The only thing keeping men here at all is the chance of a quick fortune. The heat is bad, the humidity. And if that wasn't enough we have to listen to that damn pounding, day after day, night after night. I tell you, Walker, a man would be a fool to stay here if he didn't have to."

"And yet you stay here."

"My duty lies on Venus," said Carmody stiffly. "A soldier obeys orders. He doesn't question them."

"Peters didn't stay," reminded Jeff quietly. "I knew Peters. He was a soldier, a reliable man, a man who would have stuck to the last. *What happened to Peters, Carmody?"*

For a long moment there was silence, a silence so intense that the subdued murmur of the drums seemed to come nearer, to enter the very room, bringing an impression of the raw, the savage, the utterly primeval. Carmody didn't move. He just sat and stared at Jeff with eyes like holes punched in white dough. After a long while he licked his lips and the clink of glass chattering against his teeth echoed like castanets in the throbbing silence. He drank, his throat working as he gulped, and when he set down the glass it was empty.

"Damn you, Walker," he said without anger. "Why must you keep harping on Peters? He was my commander. I saw him every day. We left Earth together. Can't you forget him?"

"No."

"He was always interested in the natives. A lot of us thought that he was too much interested. It wasn't the right thing to do. Earthmen and Venusians shouldn't mix, and yet he was the commander. We couldn't stop him."

Carmody stared down at his empty glass and spoke as if he were alone.

"I saw it happen. I saw a man rot beneath my eyes, his moral fibre vanishing as he began to turn native." Jeff winced at the scorn in the heavy voice. "We reasoned with him of course, the young captain he was friendly with, myself, some of the men, but he wouldn't listen. In the end he resigned, I still don't know just why, and now you tell me that he's as good as dead."

He stared at Jeff and his eyes were pits of torment.

"I could have stopped it, you know. I could have stopped him mingling with the savages, talking to the Shamans, lowering his entire race. It isn't good for a man to forget his dignity, Walker, to turn against his race, to betray his heritage. I did what I could of course, but that was little enough, and when the trouble came he couldn't stand it. We had to clear an area, take over a village; we even had to kill some of the natives. I knew that Peters didn't like doing what had to be done. I think his mind must have snapped, and so he resigned and I took over and finished the job."

"And Peters returned to Earth, to lie rotting in gutters, poisoned with some exotic drug?"

"So you tell me. I wouldn't know about the drug."

"I see." Jeff stared down at his glass, at the watery fluid it contained, then swallowed it quickly. "This isn't getting me anywhere. I'll be back in time to catch the rocket."

He rose, setting the empty glass down on the edge of the desk, and watching Carmody trying to hide both relief and anger. Jeff shrugged. Somehow he just didn't care a damn what Carmody felt; he didn't care a damn what anyone felt.

He'd just about had enough.

Outside, the wide leaves of the fern trees threw a shadow of deceptive coolness.

He began walking deep into the forest.

* * * *

The sounds came from a million miles away from the other side of the sun, from distant Earth, from the intangible land lying the other side of dreams. A thin chiming sound, a muted booming, a tinkling splash and a liquid rustle.

Jeff opened his eyes and listened to the sounds.

He lay on his side, his cheek pressed against the rich black loam of the forest floor, his knees bent a little and one arm doubled up beside his face. Aside from the sounds it was very quiet, and he frowned as he tried to fit them into a recognisable pattern. Then something struck his cheek with a warm dampness, and he smiled.

It was raining.

From the lowering clouds above streamed warm rain. The swollen droplets struck the wide leaves of the fern trees, bounced, fell to lower leaves, bounced again, and finally splashed to the black soil. It made a pleasant harmony of whispering noise, a peaceful sound, the whisper of nature in a world as yet unspoiled.

It lulled, soothed, washed away all care and worry, and listening to it, Jeff felt for the first time in years a sense of contentment and satisfaction. He sighed, rolled onto his back, staring up at the thick blanket of leaves and relishing the feel of the warm rain on his face.

After what seemed a long while he sat up.

Weakness gripped him, a horrible sense of utter nausea and fatigue. He stooped thrusting his head between h knees in a desperate effort to wash away the tides of blackness pressing around the edges of his vision. He groaned rolled over onto his face, gripped the loose wet soil with both hands.

Someone touched his shoulder.

He twisted, staring up at a calm face, at long white hair and intelligent eyes. The native smiled at him, and in the dim light the black markings on his body seemed to writhe and move as if they had an independent life of their own.

"You are awake," he said. "Good. Drink this now."

Weakly Jeff took the hollow gourd and gulped at the thick slimy contents. It burned his throat a little and the oiliness of the liquid made his stomach heave and churn, but he tightened his lips against the sickness, and after a little while it passed.

"What happened?" He stared wildly at the calm features of the Venusian. "Where am I?"

"You are deep in the forest, a long way from your people. You have been ill, very ill; now you must rest and rebuild your strength." He smiled and reached for the gourd. "Can you drink a little more now?"

"I'll try." Jeff forced himself to swallow the thick liquid. He tilted the gourd, letting some of it slop over his chin, gagging a little over the horrible oiliness, and yet feeling that it was doing him good.

He paused, wiping his mouth with the back of his hand, then stared, his eyes widening in horror.

His arm looked like a stick.

Thin and wasted, dead white and soggy, covered with dirt and ingrained filth. He stared down at his body, at his hollow chest and protruding ribs, his rags of clothing and the festering wounds on legs and thighs. He touched his face and his beard was a tangled mass. He felt his hair, and it hung low over his neck, the matted strands sleazy and loaded with mud.

He smelt his flesh and knew what had happened.

The same sweet sickly smell, the odour of alien things, mingled with stale perspiration and blending with the rancid odour of an unwashed animal. He thought of Peters and of what had happened to him. He remembered the condition of what had once been a man, and the memory tore at his stomach so that he vomited.

Silently the native handed him the refilled gourd.

"You must drink," he said quietly. "Unless you drink you will die." It was a cold statement of fact. Grimly he took the gourd and gulped down the noxious mess.

"You have been ill," repeated the native. "For a long time you have eaten no food. Your stomach is shrunken and must be treated with care. Your strength has vanished and must be restored. Your body was poisoned and must be cleansed."

"Poisoned?" Jeff looked sharply at the calm features of the native, and frowned. "How? When?" He gulped at the liquid mess again. "Who are you?"

"We have met before." The native stared at him, a puzzled expression in his clear albino-pink eyes. "Do you not re member me?"

"No." Jeff stared at the man, at the strange black markings and the small gourd swinging at his waist. "I remember now; there was a man, I shot him, and another one who tried to kill me." He paused, frowning with the effort of memory. "I trailed his blood and found him in the hospital. I saw the commander, and we talked for a while. He gave me a drink, then I went for a walk in the forest. Then...?"

"Do not try to recall what happened then," said the native quickly. "Blank it from your mind, ignore it. Forget that time existed between then and now."

"Why?"

"Because some things are not well to know."

"It was the drink," mused Jeff. "It must have been the drink. Carmody made too many slips; he knew about the shooting in the settlement, and yet I hadn't told him where it occurred. I was drugged, drugged the same way as Peters was drugged." He swallowed, thinking of Peters. "What will happen to me now?"

"You will live," said the Shaman quietly. "You will be weak for a time and there will be one spot in your memory that must forever remain a blank. More than that I cannot do, for your science is not as ours and your body in many ways is unpredictable."

"Then I was right—the drug does originate on Venus?"

"It does."

"Of course," Jeff said softly. "It had to originate here. Peters proved that, but..." He stared at the native. "How did it come to be in Terrestrial hands?"

"What men seek they find," said the Shaman ambiguously, "and if they seek destruction, that also will they find."

"Stop it," snapped Jeff irritably. He reached for the gourd and though his throat tightened at the touch of the liquid, he drank it down. He felt better now, not so sick, and while still horribly weak, yet his head was clear.

"You don't have to talk that way to me. I know you too well; you are an intelligent man. Did you give the drug to Peters?"

"No."

"Did he steal it?"

"Like all of his race he took what he wanted."

"Then he did steal it." Jeff rested his head on his hands, supporting his elbows on his knees. Somewhere was the one clue which eluded him, somewhere was the key to the mystery. Peters had discovered an exotic drug, and that discovery had been important enough for him to have resigned his commission and return to Earth, and yet...?

A man couldn't operate on his own back. A man couldn't imbed a container beneath skin and flesh, and what man would deliberately drug himself into the state in which Peters was found? There had to be more than one man connected with it, perhaps several men. The doctor, Carmody, the young captain who perhaps knew too much and so had to die. The natives must know about it; the stuff originated from them, and that meant trade between the races.

He looked at the Shaman. "What is the drug?"

"This?" The native touched the small gourd hanging at his waist. "We have a name for it, but your people call it Exotic. A strange name, but then you have a strange language."

"Exotic?" Jeff stared at the man, then shrugged. "One name is as good as another I suppose. What does it do?"

"Ask those who know."

"Meaning that you won't tell me." Jeff smiled a little as he stared at the calm features. "Whatever it is must be pretty bad. Remember I've seen it work, though from my own experience I can't swear to that." He frowned, trying to recall the blank spot in his mind, and for a moment nostalgia gripped him and he felt a terrible longing.

"Be warned," said the Shaman quietly. "Do not try to recall what happened. If you do, you will be as good as dead."

"Dead!" Jeff smacked his hand down onto his naked thigh. "Now I remember. You gave that injured man some just before he died—the native those Earthmen shot." He stared at the native and within his skull little wheels seemed to spin and facts fell into a composite pattern of utter simplicity.

"So that's what those men were after! Not the native at all, not even to kill you, except that it was incidental to their plan. They wanted what you carried, the gourd at your waist, the container of the drug!"

The native remained silent, his white body against the black markings almost luminous in the dimness of the forest.

"You knew that," whispered Jeff incredulously. "You knew it all the time."

"Yes."

"And that native, the one who was shot, did he know also?"

"Yes."

"I can't believe it." Jeff shook his head in bafflement. "A native walks to a place where he knows that he will be shot and killed. You follow him. You know what is going to happen and yet you still follow him. Why?"

The Shaman said nothing, just sat on the rich black loam and stared at the Terrestrial with wide, albino-pink eyes.

"Those men," continued Jeff slowly. "Now I know why I had the impression they were hunting, using the injured native as bait. All they really wanted was the gourd at your waist." He looked at the calm features of the Venusian. "You knew that?"

"Then why in Heaven's name didn't you just give it to them?"

"Would you give a child fire to play with?" The Shaman's voice was very deep as he stared at a spot somewhere beyond. "It is not for us to place into the hands of any race the means of self-destruction, and yet if they insist, who are we to deny them their destiny? In this matter we are without guilt. We have not done as you tried to do. We have not bribed you with drink and drugs, cheap goods and pitiful substitutes for correct living. We have not robbed you of what is yours, then thrown you crumbs as compensation. We have done none of these things. Why then are we to blame?"

"You are not to blame. No one said that you were."

"If we had given you the drug, then we should have been guilty, and that is something not to be borne. No. Your own people discovered the drug. Your own race found out what it was and why it was used. Earthmen decided that it was what they wanted, and so they took it as they take everything they think they need. They took it with the violence of their weapons. They took it with murder and with blood and with hate. So be it."

"I'm beginning to understand," whispered Jeff. He shuddered at the alien philosophy, the calm acceptance that men had to die so that an alien race could take what they wanted. "You deliberately offered yourself to be shot down, knowing that those men would take the drug." He stiffened as a thought stabbed at his brain, and his mouth went dry as he remembered Peters and just what the drug could do.

"What is the drug?"

The Shaman said nothing, his eyes blank windows of hidden thought.

"What is the drug?"

"Death," said the native, and smiled. Silence closed around them as the word whispered to nothing in the dim forest

* * * *

The silence grew, deepened, and closed around them with thick consistency. The rain had stopped, even the fairy bells of the falling droplets had ceased, and in the sudden hush Jeff became aware of something missing.

The drums.

At first he hardly noticed. Then, so ingrained had the regular cadence become, he actively missed the steady pounding of the monotonous rhythm. He shifted a little on the soft loam; then, fastening on the minor thing as relief from what he had just heard, mentioned it to the Shaman.

"Yes," said the native calmly. "We no longer need them. It is unnecessary to retain the barrier."

"Barrier?"

"Yes."

Jeff shrugged, then returned to things of immediate importance.

"You said the drug was death," he reminded. "Did you mean that literally?"

"The drug is not poisonous if that is what you mean. In itself it is harmless; its potency lies in the effect it has on the brain."

"Madness?"

"No."

"Then what, or don't you want to tell me?"

The Shaman stared at him, his eyes glazed a little as if he were listening to something far away; then he relaxed, the black markings on his body writhing a little as the muscles rippled beneath his skin.

"We are an old race," he said abruptly, "a race older than perhaps you can imagine. We also have had our childish troubles, our wars, our attempts at improving on the natural way of life, but always we returned to sanity, and now we are as you see us."

"Primitive?" Jeff stared at the superb body of the native, the intelligent eyes and the cleanliness of mind and body. He shook his head. "No. You are not savages. Perhaps that is why we hate you so much."

"Perhaps. It is natural for one race to fight against the superiority of another, but enough of that. We learned long ago that the mind is a delicate thing, and we also learned that thought has power. So we turned our back on things which disturbed the natural rhythm of life and concentrated instead on inner wellbeing. We succeeded."

"What has all this got to do with the drug?"

"Naturally we discovered things. The use of fire. The ways of the forest. The fundamental principles of vibration. We learned the use of many plants, of herbs, of natural medicine. Some of what we learned had immediate application; other things seemed to be of little use, while still others were pregnant with danger. And yet all knowledge is of use, so we did not discard anything."

"The drug was one such discovery?"

"Yes. The drug you call Exotic was one such thing. Dangerous, and yet still with its uses."

"In which way?"

"Each man must die," said the Shaman quietly. "Every living being must sooner or later embark on the final journey.

Sometimes the passing is one of peace, at others wrought with pain and fear. Old men die and young, but all die. It is then we use the drug."

"Why?"

"What is life?" said the native quietly. "Is it a struggle, a battle to grab all you can while you can? Or is it a calm acceptance of what is and must be? What is ambition? What is hope? What is fear and the futile longing for the unattainable? What is death?"

"For each of these questions there must be a different answer," said Jeff sombrely. "Your race and mine could never agree on a definition."

"Exactly. Each man has his own idea of what life should be, and so arises discord. The drug puts an end to all that."

"How?"

"If a man knew that he could have whatever he wanted, satisfy his wildest ambition and every craving, if he knew that he would have all this, would he still struggle with his fellows?"

"I don't know," said Jeff. "Some men are never satisfied, can never be satisfied. No matter how much they have they still want more."

"Remember I said everything they want. The men you speak of do not have that, always there must be something they need, some object they cannot attain. If they could each experience their own heaven, would there still be strife?"

"I think there would. Men aren't built to be satisfied. Logically the Earth can produce sufficient for all, and yet still some starve while other waste. Logic has nothing to do with mankind."

"Then what has?"

"Greed perhaps? Personal ambition, the lust for power, the desire to be strong? Some men crave the adulation of others, some the love of women. Still others worship tokens, forgetting what the true reality is." Jeff shook his head. "I cannot answer your question. Men have sought an answer since first they learned to think. They are still seeking an answer. They haven't found it and I don't believe they ever will."

"You are wrong," the Shaman said quietly. "Men have found the answer."

"The drug?"

"The drug."

Silence closed around them again, the silence of thought and unanswerable questions. A leaf fell softly from one of the trees and the rustle of its passage echoed like the thin whispers of the dead. Jeff shuddered, his body feeling an unfamiliar chill.

"You called it 'death'," he whispered. "Why did you call it that?"

"A race is as strong as an individual of that race, no stronger. If the individual is weak, then the race is weak; if strong, then the race will endure. Men are weak."

"And Venusians are strong?"

"We are stronger than you."

"I believe it," said Jeff dully. "I have seen men corrupted by wealth, and I have seen the trade goods rotting in the store. I have seen men turn native, but I have not yet seen a Venusian turn Terrestrial. Somehow I think that we have failed, but it took an alien race to show us just where we failed. Men will reach the stars, but who will mourn them when they are gone?"

"There is still hope for your race while it produces men who can think as you do." The Shaman reached for the gourd and poured more of the noxious liquid. Silently he passed the gourd and silently Jeff drank it down.

"What is the drug?"

"Desire made concrete. Ambition fulfilled. Dreams made real and longings satisfied. It is the ultimate in euphoria—and it is death."

"And yet you use it?" Jeff put down the empty gourd. "Why is that?"

"Why should we spurn it? Think. A man is hovering on the edge of the great dark, trembling on the first step of the long journey. What harm can it do, then? We come when we are called, and to the one who calls we give the drug. It banishes pain, destroys fear, provides comfort. It divorces the mind from the body, alters the time sense, allows a man to experience to the ultimate every desire and longing, every hope and ambition. What he thinks, is. What he imagines, comes true. Mentally, physically, in utter sublimation of logic and sense, he lives a dream and to him that dream is real."

"Dope," said Jeff, and for the first time began to understand. "Cocaine, opium, marijuana, all have in a minor way the same effect. They divorce the addict from reality, enable him to live in a fantastic world of his own. So the drug is just dope, and yet you call it 'death.' You are wrong. Mankind has lived with it for too long to be ruined by anything you can produce. We have too many poisons of our own."

"I agree," said the native, and if he had been from Earth Jeff would have suspected him of irony. "You have too many poisons."

"Then why should your drug be so deadly?"

"Why do men come to Venus? Why do they work and suffer in a climate which to them must be oppressive, under conditions barren of comfort, without the society of their kind? Why do men reach for the stars? Why do they war, lie, cheat, steal, kill their enemies and betray their friends? What makes your civilisation? What is the one great driving force of your race?"

"Money," said Jeff, and knew that he spoke the truth. "Tokens. But why are they so important?"

"Because of the power they represent. Because of what they can do, the things they can buy, the comfort they can produce."

"Then if all those things could be had without constant, strife, would men still work, still reach for the stars, still war and struggle?"

"I don't know. Money, as you say, is merely a means to an end, but some men worship it for itself alone."

"Yet those men are few, and if money was valueless would they be regarded as sane?"

"No."

"Well?"

Jeff stared at the calm features of the oddly marked native. He looked at the great boles of the fern trees, dim in the shadow of their wide leaves. He touched the rich black soil, then finally faced the inevitable fact.

The Shaman was right!

The drug was death. Death to all hope and ambition, to struggle and progress, to wasted dreams and futile desire. He imagined Peters, a man so engrossed in his dreams that he had forgotten to eat, forgotten to bathe, forgotten that he was a man. He had stumbled through the gutters, lost in his dream world, and while his feet trod filth yet his mind roved the distant places between the stars.

Perhaps he had been a king ruling over a nation of beautiful women. Perhaps he had ruled all Earth and turned it into a Utopia. Perhaps he had made wonderful discoveries in the realms of science. They would never know, for a man's dreams were sacred and peculiar to himself alone.

But the wakening must have been hell.

To return to the harsh world of reality. To smell the dirt and feel the hunger. To see the hard faces of men and the empty eyes of women, to be nothing, to be less than the dirt beneath the wheels of humming turbine cars. Could any man stand it for long? Could he stand the frustration, the bleakness, the constant struggle for food and shelter, the search for friends? Could he stand it when all he had to do was to take a pinch of power and return to his private kingdom?

Jeff knew he couldn't.

No man could. No man born of woman could deny himself the culmination of all he had ever worked and hoped for, all he had dreamed and wished for. It took too much, demanded too much. It was replacing heaven with hell—and men were weak.

The drug was truly death.

He had a vision of Earth peopled with blank-eyed men and women. People who had tasted of the exotic escape of alien drugs. They would shamble through deserted, streets or lie supine on unmade beds. Children would whimper for mothers surrounded by a world of imaginary lovers or fathers immersed in their own private harems. The factories would whine to a stop, the crops rot in the fields; the animals would die, then the people, falling in the streets, starving while gorging themselves on imaginary banquets, rotting from disease while enjoying imaginary health. It had happened to Peters, it could happen to the world.

Men were weak.

He drew a shuddering breath; then, like a tiny flame, hope blossomed somewhere deep inside him. He grinned, forcing stiff lips into a stiff mask, and for a moment felt the wild thrill of conquest and exultation.

The drug was deadly—but *he had been drugged!*

"I found you soon after," said the Shaman softly. "I followed you until the poison had worked its course. I tended you, watched over you—and I cleansed your mind of memories."

"Cleansed my mind?"

"Yes. If I had not, you would be in the grip of such craving as you could never imagine. You would be tormented by the world you had lost, the world fashioned of dreams and suppressed desires. Nothing would matter to you but one thing—to regain that world in any way possible. You would have killed me for what I carry at my waist. You would plunge your world into war, kill your friends, do anything. For nothing would be important except what you had tasted and lost."

"So you say," gritted Jeff defiantly. "But how can you tell?"

"Why do you think we only give the drug at the moment of death? Why do you think that only we who are marked as I am marked carry the drug? Strong as we are, yet we are only as strong as ourselves, and the drug is as strong as desire, which is stronger than all." The Shaman paused and Jeff could sense a great sadness and an unbearable longing.

"We are tested, we who wear the black. Tested as few men can be tested. For we hold a great trust and one not to be abused. We know of what we do, know it the only way possible."

"You have tasted the drug," said Jeff. "You have entered this world of dreams."

"Yes."

Suddenly it began to rain, a whispering patter of swollen drops drumming against the leaves with muted thunder. It grew darker, the shadows seeming to cluster around the boles of the great trees. The native rose and Jeff rose with him.

Together they walked through the forest.

* * * *

The high wire fence surrounding the landing field glimmered like a jewel-encrusted web, the huddle of shacks like a heap of discarded filth. Jeff paused at the edge of the settlement and narrowed his eyes at the utter lack of motion, the absence of life, the pregnant stillness hanging over the area. He strode through the semi-liquid between the huts, peering inside some of them, then halted before the locked gate of the compound.

A red-eyed guard stared at him, the long barrel of his high-velocity rifle swinging down as he searched the forest with tired eyes.

"Open up," snapped Jeff. He leaned against the wire as the guard fumbled with the lock, cursing the weakness which even after two weeks of native feeding still tore at his body. Grimly he stumbled through the gate and headed for the administration buildings.

Carmody waited for him in the office.

The commander looked a wreck. His small eyes glowed against the pallor of his features, his hair was a tangled mass, and a heavy stubble coated lips and chin. He stared at Jeff as if he were seeing a ghost, then slumped back in his chair, his shoulders rounded and sagging with something more than just fatigue.

"Remember me, Carmody?" Jeff almost fell into a chair. "Walker. I came to investigate drug smuggling. Remember?"

"Yes. Yes, I remember you."

"Didn't expect to see me again, did you?"

"Sure I expected to see you again. I'd have sent out a search party, but things came up and I couldn't."

"What sort of things, Carmody?"

"Little things. We'll get over it. We always have. It just takes a little time."

"Time?" Jeff shook his head. "No, Carmody. Time won't cure it." He paused, watching the slow revolutions of the electric fan. "I passed by the mining site," he said gently. "I looked inside some of the huts. I counted your soldiers. Something's gone wrong, hasn't it, Carmody? Something's backfired right in your face."

"I don't know what you're talking about."

"Don't you?" Jeff shrugged and reached for a cigarette. He shook one from the package, then threw it back onto the wide desk. "A native found me," he said conversationally. "A Shaman. He looked after me, fed me, told me a few things. I know all about it, Carmody. I know what happened to Peters."

"You do?" The commander relaxed a little, and his hand fell from the open drawer at his side. "What did happen?"

Jeff didn't answer, just sat and stared at the sweating figure of the commander, letting thin streamers of blue smoke spill from his nostrils.

"I learned quite a bit while I was away," he said. "I learned that the natives are telepathic. I know why they use drums. And I know where the drug comes from."

"You know a lot," sneered the commander. "Sometimes a man can know just a little too much."

"Like that young officer who died. Peters' friend—did he know too much?"

"I don't know what you're talking about."

"I'm talking about Venus, about a new world just ripe for the picking, about men who let the glitter of gold dazzle them to reality, and who forget they are men. I'm talking about Peters, a man who tried to learn something, and who learned too much. I'm talking about all those men out in the huts, the blank-eyed men, the drugged men, the men who've finally found what they have been searching for all their lives."

He leaned forward and crushed out the butt of the cigarette.

"I'm talking about a rat!"

"I don't like what you say, Walker. Remember where you are and what I am."

"You're a fool, Carmody, the biggest fool on two planets." Jeff surged to his feet and strode about the room. "Man didn't you realise that you were at war? Didn't it ever occur to you that perhaps the Venusians might not like the idea of you taking over their world? That they might hit back?"

"You're insane!" Carmody shrugged and reached for a bottle pouring himself out a drink. He didn't offer one to his visitor.

"Am I?"

"Yes. What could those animals out there do? What weapons have they? How could they win any sort of war?"

"They've won it," said Jeff quietly, and sat down, cursing the weakness tearing at his body.

"They learned something from us, Carmody. They learned our one great weakness, and once they learned that we couldn't win. They learned that men are basically weak, and the rest was inevitable."

"Yes?"

"Yes. Who told you of the drug? Who first gave you the idea that it was just the thing to smuggle to Earth? How did you hope to keep the secret to yourself?"

"Are you accusing me of smuggling?"

"Yes, and I can prove it."

Carmody grinned, his lips drawing back from his teeth in an ugly snarl. His hand dipped into the drawer and when it reappeared he held a gun. Jeff stared at the tiny orifice of the high-velocity pistol and shrugged.

"Going to kill me, Carmody?"

"Why not? I never did like snoops."

"You won't kill me," said Jeff quietly. "I have friends out there, the natives, and if you kill me they'll know it. I told you they were telepathic, remember. Those drums were just to blanket out our disorganised thought, a form of barrier between us and them. If you kill me they'll leave the area—*and you won't get any more of the drug!*"

"I don't need it."

"Yes you do, and you know it. What happened while I was away? What blew up during those three weeks I wandered the forest, lost in the mist of that dope you slipped into my drink? Did he talk? The man whose hand I ruined? The secret was too good to keep after all, wasn't it? Why get drunk when there was something far better to hand? Did they raid your store, Carmody? Did they help themselves? Is that what happened?"

"I couldn't stop them," the commander said dully. "I tried but my own men betrayed me. They acted as if they were crazy. I warned them, but it did no good." The gun made a flat metallic sound as it fell back into the drawer. "God help me, Walker, what can I do?"

"Nothing."

"Nothing?"

"Not a single thing. I told you that the natives had won, and they have. Almost every Terrestrial on the planet is in a drugged stupor. You know what will happen when they come out of it. The Shamans won't be around to let themselves get shot for the sake of what they carry. You are the only place they can get the stuff from, and remember, nothing will stop them getting it."

"I know," whispered the commander. "I know."

"Peters must have discovered what the drug was for. He was curious, probably, persuaded them to give him some, or maybe his friend 'found' some for him. There is a way to test the effects of narcotics. You dissolve some in alcohol, then spray it through an atomiser. That way you can test the effects without much danger of becoming an addict."

Jeff shrugged and reached for the cigarettes.

"He didn't know what he was doing."

"I was with him when he tried it," said Carmody sickly. "He used far too strong a dose; it got him immediately. When he came out of it nothing would stop him trying it again. The effects lasted about an hour, so he didn't get too weak. I fixed it with one of the pilots to arrange a contact on Earth. I knew what the stuff would bring in the right quarters. Peters was the third carrier we used. The doc was in on it of course. He did the operation."

"So you got Peters to take a big dose, shipped him out, and promised further supplies when he delivered." Jeff nodded, his eyes hidden behind drifting veils of smoke.

"You knew that he couldn't resist, that he would do anything to get more. I said you were a rat, Carmody. I'm sorry, I didn't intend to insult an animal."

"You don't have to act so damn superior," snarled the commander. "You would have done the same in my place. Hell, man, who wants to stick in this god-forsaken hole when he could be back home? You know how long I've got to stop here? You know what my pay is? I saw a chance to get what I wanted and I took it. Where's the harm? A few natives shot. Who will worry about them? A few too-rich reprobates on Earth kick off sooner than expected, who cares? Take me in if you want to; I've done a little smuggling, so what? Two, three years and I'll be out of jail and working again, and brother, with what I know I can get my own ship."

"That," said Jeff grimly, "was just what I was afraid of."

He dropped the cigarette and trod on it. He rose from his chair and, before the commander could stop him, had scooped up the pistol. He poised it in his hand and his eyes were hard and cold, like steel and ice.

"You're not going back to Earth, Carmody. No one is going back who has tasted that drug. This entire area is under quarantine."

"You're crazy!"

"No. I'm not the one who is crazy. You are. Can't you see what could happen? Can't you see the effects that drug will have? Hasn't it struck you yet that these Venusians are serious? They knew what you would do. They knew that they would be shot for what they carried, and yet they deliberately walked to their death. Their twisted ethics made it impossible for them to give us the stuff. If we wanted it we had to take it, and we did. Would Earthmen have done that? Would Earthmen have' kept a secret so well?"

"I don't understand."

"Look at it this way. If they had given us the drug we would have been suspicious. We would have tested it, banned it, warned the men against it. But they didn't do that. No. We had to be clever. We had to find out for ourselves. We had to reason that the natives didn't know about the drug and that we had to lure them like game in order to be killed so that we could get it. That made it legal, That made everything all right."

Jeff almost quivered with anger, the gleaming barrel of the pistol trembling in his hand.

"Can you imagine a race like that? Think about it for a moment. Can you?"

A sickly expression glazed the commander's eyes and drew his features down into sagging folds. He stared at Jeff with horror, and when he spoke his voice seemed to fight its way through a pile of mush.

"My God," he whispered. "How they must hate us!"

Slowly Jeff nodded and let the pistol fall to his side.

"Yes," he said. "They hate us, and yet their hate is a peculiar thing. I would call it determination rather than hate. They know that we will contaminate the planet and so they did something to stop us. If we return there will be something else, and then something else after that. We can't win, Carmody; we're out of our class and the sooner we realise it the better. Man is no longer the Lord Of Creation. Other races have their own right to live s they want to. It's a lesson we had to learn, and we must learn it before we can really say that we are ready for the stars."

"What is going to happen then? What of us?"

"Those who have used the drug will die. They will return to reality and crave their dream world again. I have the Shaman's promise that supplies of the drug will be given to them. Within two or three months they will be dead—nothing can alter that."

"Why? You were drugged and you are still alive." Hope glowed deep in the small eyes. "There must be an antidote! You found it. Tell me that you found it!"

"I found no antidote." Jeff stared at the commander's glittering eyes. "So it has got you too," he said wonderingly. "Knowing what it can do to a man, still you couldn't resist it." He stared at the man with something almost akin to pity. "You poor fool! There is no antidote. The Shaman worked on my mind, blanketed my memory, wiped out what heaven I must have experienced while wandering in the forest. He did it for me, but he won't do it for anyone else."

"Why not? You could make him, threaten to kill him if he didn't. Walker, you've got to help me! You've got to help me!"

"No. I was treated for a specific reason. You must die with the rest."

"No!"

"Yes. I am to be the spokesman. I have agreed to a treaty. We are to have all this area, a hundred square miles, no more, and in return we respect their right to own their own world. No further supplies of the drug will be available while we keep to the treaty, but if we break it…"

"They are savages. You can't consider them against one of your own. I don't want to die, Walker. I want to live, to enjoy all the things I never had time for or could never get. Life is too short, it's over too soon. A man is old before he gets anywhere and then it's too late."

"Then take some of your own drug," snapped Jeff, and strode from the room.

Outside he waited for a moment, waited while a semi-hysterical man fumbled in drawers and found what he had searched for all his life. Glass clinked and something sighed as it rested on the floor. Jeff hesitated, stared at the blank-eyed man lying on the plastic flooring, a blank-eyed man now lost in a private world of dreams, then slowly left the office for the second time.

Outside clouds piled up in the sky, dimming the golden patch of the hidden sun. A thin breeze rustled the wide leaves of the great trees and a guard stared curiously at him as he stood by the gate.

He felt very tired.

There was so much to do, men to take care of, others to evict from the wired area. The ships would come and leave again, until ships from Earth would arrive with new and different personnel. Venus would still provide a halting place for the travel hungry men of Earth, but now men would respect it, treat it as a world should be treated, and one day…

One day Terrestrial and Venusian would meet and each call the other friend. The two races would mingle, would share what they possessed, would mount the long road to the stars together, each helping the other. Time would pass and old wounds be healed, but it would take a lot of time.

A lot of time, but it would happen.

Gently, it began to rain.

THE TOUCH OF REALITY

In his youth he had dreamt of the Moon and all it wonders—but not of this nightmare journey stalked by death at every turn.

Few dreams can stand the touch of reality. When he was young Mark Sturent had often stared through a quarter of a million miles of air and vacuum at the shining face of the moon. It had attracted him as it had all boys of imagination and he had built up a mental fantasy of brave adventure and heroic endeavour, picturing a little community of men facing, and surmounting, an almost hopeless challenge with himself, naturally, as one of the leaders. Now, twenty years later, reality had soured the dream.

Seen at close quarters the moon was not a pleasant place. It was too harsh, too sterile, too cold at night and too hot during the day. The craters were death traps of mist-fine dust; the mountains jagged and rotten like the crumbling teeth of a skull. It was too quiet, too lonely, too much like the ravaged face of a long dead woman who yearned for company in her dissolution. Even the Earthlight did little to soften the barren bleakness and the stars, bright and unwavering, hung like frozen snowdrops in the sky.

But if the brave adventure and heroic endeavour had vanished the challenge remained. It was a very simple challenge and a very personal one. It was the ability to stay alive, Mark, sprawled in his suit, sometimes wondered just how long he would be able to meet and defeat it. So far he had been lucky.

"Coffee," whispered a voice from the helmet radio. "Man! Could I use a cup of Java!"

That would be Sam Levine, young, brash, supremely self-confident, cynical as only a man who has never evaluated life can be cynical. He knew the price of everything, the worth of nothing and adhered to the credo of self, first, last and all the time. He was devoid of imagination and could stare at the beauty of Earth, compare it to the surface of the moon and his only thought would be for a hot dog, a cup of coffee and a cigarette thrown in for good measure.

"Button it up," said Mark into his microphone. "No talking."

"Hell, Cap, why not?" Sam sounded aggrieved. "Just staying out here doing nothing, saying nothing, is giving me the willies."

"You heard what I said." Mark squinted at the luminous face of the chronometer set among an array of instruments just above his viewport. "Melkin?"

"Here. Captain." Carl sounded disapproving. Mark guessed that had he been in charge of the patrol he would have blasted Sam for breaking radio silence—and probably done more harm by his tirade than that caused by the original fault.

"How are you feeling?" Mark smiled to himself at what Carl must be thinking. He, the Captain, breaking his own firm injunction against any but routine radio contact.

"I'm fine. Captain." The note of disapproval was now more in evidence.

"Not too cold?"

"No, sir."

"Levine?"

"I'm freezing." Sam made his teeth chatter to accentuate his complaint. "How much longer we got to stay out here, Cap?"

"Not much longer." Mark glanced again at the chronometer. "Relax, Sam, that coffee will taste all the better for having had to wait for it."

"Maybe." Sam didn't sound convinced. He would have said more but Mark forestalled him.

"No more talking. Keep your eyes peeled and your mouth shut."

It was the old injunction repeated, Mark didn't know how often, but as important now as it had ever been. Watch, don't talk! For talking, via radio, could be picked up and a directional fix taken. And betrayal of their position could mean a bullet-punctured suit or worse. For, in this strangest of all wars, neither side was playing.

It was a war which was officially unrecognised, a struggle which was not apparent on Earth or more than suspected by other; than the interested parties. It was a war with peculiar rules and a specific code which had nothing to do with chivalry but everything to do with survival. To bomb the main bases would have been simple but would have led to immediate retaliation and global conflict. To destroy the ships prior to landing would not have been too difficult but would have been tantamount to suicide. It was a war with an unwritten agreement that neither side would destroy inexpendable material. But men were not inexpendable.

Which was why Captain Mark Sturent rested on the Luna dust in the Luna night, eyes staring towards the enemy sector and a mark IV machine rifle at his side.

Waiting is hard at the best of times and waiting in the narrow confines of a space suit is the hardest of all. Bodily functions have to be suspended or, if not, the discomfort increases. The limbs are hampered by the tight fitting plastic, the head enclosed in the great, globular helmet, and life balances on the ability of the bodily heat, plus electrical battery power to combat heat loss by radiation so that survival is possible at -240 F.

Lying in his suit Mark wondered, not for the first time, just what had ever made him think of the moon as a place of romance. Coupled with the fear that his power would fail and leave him to freeze in the cold of the Luna night was the uneasy knowledge that his life depended on the smooth functioning of his air unit. If it failed then he would die. If it continued to function then he would draw breath as long as he could live. The closed cycle algae system had been the greatest weapon in the battle against the environment. But even with air and heat the psychological factor posed a problem.

"Cap." It was Sam again. "I think I've spotted something."

"Where?" Mark was instantly alert.

"Over by the triple peak. About one-fifteen. See it?"

"Melkin?" Mark wasted no time. From his own position he had a bad view of the named position but Carl would have it in his field of vision.

"Nothing." Melkin was very positive. "Sam just wants hear the sound of his own voice."

"I don't want to hear the sound of yours," said Mark sharply. "Keep watching, you too Sam, and report only if you've anything definite."

Cautiously he wriggled to a point of better vantage, rolling his body so that his viewport pointed in the right direction. He blinked, stared and was not too surprised to find that he saw no signs of anything suspicious. But he didn't allow himself to relax.

It might be a false alarm, probably was, or, even, it was as Carl had suggested and Sam wanted to hear the sound of human voices. Locked in a suit, away from even the sight of a companion, it wasn't too hard for a man to slip into the illusion that he was wholly alone. It was natural for such a man to want to hear that others were alive and around him. Natural enough for him to even have a hallucination to justify his breaking radio silence.

Or maybe he had actually seen something and was telling the simple truth.

Mark had never actually met the enemy. He had seen signs of their presence, examined their footsteps in the dust and made abortive attempts to track them to their base, but that was all. As far as he knew the enemy had never seen him either, the fact of his existence was proof of that, but there was always a first time for everything and, for all Mark knew, this could be his first time. He wanted to make certain that it wouldn't be his last.

Movement, in the pressure suit, was not easy. Even with the one-sixth Luna gravity strengthening his muscles the journey was no pleasant stroll. Care had to be taken not to slip into a dust-filled pocket or fall from the sudden yielding of rotten stone. It took a long time for Mark to rise from his place of concealment, work his way along in the shadows until he had reached the suspected area, and assure himself that nothing lurked where Sam had said.

"Cap." Sam's voice echoed from the radio. "I can see it again."

"How many?"

"One."

"What's he doing?" Mark raised his arms as far as they would go, which was a little above his shoulders. "Well?"

"Surrendering, I think." Sam sounded doubtful. His doubt was registered in the little metallic sounds coming from the radio, the transmitted sounds of something being lifted into position and tapping against the air unit and helmet. "Should I let him have it?"

"You're looking at me, you dope," said Mark quickly; "See? I'm lowering my arms."

"Can you spot any footprints, Captain?" Carl was practical.

"No." Mark stared at the landscape, brilliantly-lit in the Earthlight, sombrely dark in the shadow. "Not a sign."

"I knew it." Carl sounded disgusted. "Sam got scared and wanted someone to hold his hand." It was, thought Mark, a good diagnosis. Sam was quickly defensive.

"I'll hold your hand, you squarehead," he snapped. "You trying to get me into trouble, or something? I tell you I saw something out there."

"Sure." Carl was sarcastic. "A Moonman, maybe?"

"Skip it." Mark felt that the argument was getting out of hand. "Maybe you did see something, Sam, and maybe you only thought that you did, but one thing is for sure. When we get back to camp you're going to spend a few hours rubbing up on recognition. You should have spotted who I was by my suit."

"At that distance?"

"You are close enough to see the movements of my arms," reminded Mark. He glanced at his instruments, the investigation had taken longer than he thought. "Better get over to Carl's position. I'll rendezvous with you there. It's time we headed back."

The best part of any patrol was, to Mark, the return to camp. It wasn't much, the camp, but it was a place where it was possible to relax. Gouged out of the side of a mountain, a combination of natural fissure and artificial cave, sealed, insulated, studded with U.V. lamps and with pine-scented air it was the acme of comfort to a man just back from patrol.

Comfort is relative. To those fortunate enough to be in Main Base the intermediate bases were places of hardship devoid of swimming pools, live theatres, shopping centres and the transported luxury of modern life. To the residents of the intermediate base the advance camps were little more than glorified jails. To the men who were attached to them they were home.

The others were together when Mark reached the rendezvous point. They touched helmets and spoke by conduction, switching off the suit radios.

"Do we return by the same route, Cap?" Sam was eager to get back to his animal comforts, he had a heap of glossy girly magazines and a deadline to make before he passed them on.

"That wouldn't be wise," said Carl before Mark could answer. "For all we know they could be waiting for us."

"I wasn't asking you," said Sam. He was still annoyed at Carl. "How about it, Cap? A quick trip for a change?"

"A safe trip," said Mark. He glanced at the chronometer. "We've got plenty of time. We'll take it slow and easy and arrive all in one piece. I'll lead, Sam will take second and Carl will cover the rear. Keep well away from the dust and stay in shadow. No talking unless you have to." He stepped away, breaking the contact before the others could argue.

Return to camp was simple and yet, in some ways, more dangerous than any other event during patrol. They were heading towards safety and that, in itself, tended to lead to carelessness. And there was more need on the return journey for watchful caution than at any other time.

The camps and intermediate bases were disguised and camouflaged for a very good reason. They were expendable targets. It was always possible that an enemy patrol had spotted them, were waiting their chance and, rather than make a quick but minor victory, gambled on hitting the jackpot, the total destruction of the advance camp. So it was vital that any returning patrol made quite certain that it wasn't being followed. Elementary caution dictated taking a different route inward than outward, but breaking new ground on the moon is always hazardous.

Mark led the way, testing spots of shadow, keeping to naked rock, taking a swinging path which would, eventually, end at the camp. Behind him, waiting until he was well ahead, came Sam. Carl waited, watching to make sure nothing was wrong, then he too advanced. It was slow going, careful going but essential.

As always, and despite his trained caution, Mark's thoughts flew ahead to their homecoming. They would group and advance to give the recognition signals. A man would come out to meet them and, if satisfied, would escort them to the disguised airlock. Once inside the camp helpers would divest them of their suits. Mark would make his report to Colonel Westerlain and then head for the spray showers. Then food, hot coffee, a taped show, books or a quiet, friendly game of chess with Latimer or Blanchard. Then rest followed by a spell of camp duty, outside guard duty, escort duty and patrol duty again.

He stumbled as rock yielded beneath his foot and caught his balance with a painful twisting of his body. The near-fall jerked him back to full awareness of his immediate surroundings and he halted, resting as he searched the landscape with his eyes. Nothing. Nothing but the inevitable dust, the jagged mountains, the broken and shattered foothills. He twisted, watched as first Sam and then Carl headed towards him and, when they had assembled, gestured for contact.

"Anything wrong?" Carl's breath sounded laboured.

"No. Just a routine check. Air units O.K.?"

"Mine is." Sam grinned through his viewport, Mark could just see his pale features grimacing behind the plastic.

"Good. Carl?"

"No trouble, Captain."

"Sure? You seem to be having trouble with your breathing."

"I almost fell back there. Then I had to hurry to catch up." Carl sounded grieved, as if Mark should have known better than to doubt his word.

"All right. Sam, you take the lead. Carl, you take second and I'll cover." Mark gestured towards a low ridge of rock some little distance ahead. "We haven't far to go now. Once over that ridge and we'll be in sighting distance of camp. Don't break your neck running."

"Coffee," said Sam. "I can taste it now." Then he was off, machine rifle at his side, his bloated torso and slender limbs giving him the appearance of some ungainly insect as he headed towards the ridge. Mark waited until he was well away, then clapped Carl on the shoulder. Alone, he turned and stared back the way they had come.

Nothing, of course, he hadn't expected anything. Sometimes he wondered, at times like this, what he would do if he did happen to spot a shape in an unfamiliar suit. Would he lurk in ambush ready and eager to kill? Would he try to take a prisoner? Would he be subtle and wait and follow so as to wipe out a thriving fleck of life on the barren moon, stamp out a tiny community of planetary brothers? It was easy for others to talk, to tell him what he should do, where his duty lay, but, secretly, Mark hoped that he would never have to make the decision. He turned a second before his rafio screamed into life.

"Cap." It was Sam, his voice thin with hysteria. "Cap, for God's sake!"

"No talking!" Mark lunged forward, safety almost forgotten in the emergency. "Save t until I reach you."

"But…"

"Shut your mouth!" Mark felt a helpless anger at the other man. He could order but that was all, obedience was something else. "Talk again and I'll shoot you on sight. I mean it!"

The threat worked. Mark raced forward, catching up with Carl just before they both reached the top of the ridge where Sam was standing. Mark reached him, knocked him over the lip of the ridge and flung himself to the ground, his helmet clanging against that of the other man.

"Fool! What's the idea of standing like a target at a shooting gallery?" Mark's ears rang as Carl thrust his helmet into contact.

"Captain!"

"I'm talking to Sam." At that moment Mark hated them both. "To pull a stupid trick like that so near to the camp…."

"Never mind that," yelled Carl. "Captain, have you seen it?"

"Seen what?"

"What I was trying to tell you." Sam swore with helpless anger. "You didn't give me no chance to tell you, no chance at all. Look!"

He lifted his arm and pointed towards a rolling cloud of dust.

* * * *

Sometimes, when tragedy comes, it is so overwhelming that it brings its own anaesthetic. Mark stared at the new-made crater, raw and angry in the Earthlight, tilted his head to stare at the last traces of the dust cloud and felt as if he were living in a dream, that none of this was real.

"It must have been recent," said Carl. His voice was strained as it echoed from the radio. "The dust hadn't even settled."

"It wouldn't." Mark kicked at a shattered scrap of debris, watching the dust plume and hover. There was no air to support it but there wasn't much gravity to pull it down again either. "From the looks of things there was an explosion and a big one at that. Anything with the force necessary to smash the camp would have thrown the dust really high. It could have happened just after we'd left."

"Gone!" Sam sounded as if he still couldn't believe it. "Just a hole in the ground."

"The enemy." Carl sounded convinced. "They must have done it." Despite his conviction he didn't bother to keep radio silence and Mark couldn't blame him. They all needed the comfort of conversation now as never before.

"They could still be out there, watching us, just waiting to let us have it." Sam's voice rose towards hysteria. "Cap, we just can't stand here, we've got to do something!"

"Take it easy." Mark took a deep breath, feeling the numbness of shock dissipate beneath the need for action. He switched off his radio, gestured and they touched helmets. "No need to take chances," he said. "We can't be sure that the enemy were responsible for this, it could have been due to an accident or natural causes."

"It wasn't an accident," insisted Carl doggedly. "If it wasn't the enemy then where are the guards?"

It was a good question. Three guards were posted at all times to watch the approaches to the camp. They should have spotted the returning patrol and challenged them.

"We'll search for the guards," said Mark. "Combat approach. Move slowly and carefully and take no chances."

"You think that we'll find them?" Sam was pathetically eager.

"No," said Carl. "We won't find the guards." Mark wished that he didn't sound so certain.

They didn't find the guards. They didn't find their bodies or any trace of the three men but that wasn't too surprising. If a man fell, or were thrown, into a dust-filled crater then he would vanish for eternity. Quicksand had nothing on the dust, it was as fine as mist, loosely packed, and a man thrown into it would disappear as a stone in water.

"That settles it," said Carl when they had re-established contact after their barren search. "They're dead and buried or taken prisoner."

"Not necessarily." Mark felt it important that he should not take anything for granted. "They could have escaped injury when the camp blew up and decided to make it to Marigold."

"Without waiting for us?" Carl was sceptical. "Sorry, Captain, but I can't agree with your theory."

"You aren't here to agree with my theories," snapped Matk. "You're here to obey orders." His sudden irritation surprised him, the shock must have been greater than he had realised. "As I see it there are at least two explanations for what has happened here. The camp could have been wrecked by accident or natural causes. In that case the guards could have decided to make it to Marigold, Or the camp could have been destroyed by the enemy. In that case the guards could have been surprised, killed and buried or disposed in some other way."

"That I can follow," said Sam. "A rocket launcher could have taken care of the camp. But why should the guards have left without waiting for us?"

"It's just possible that they were in camp when it happened," said Mark. "Or they may have assumed that the enemy were responsible, that we had been ambushed and that there was no point in their staying."

"I prefer my own explanation," said Carl stiffly. "It is neither sense nor logic to look for unreasonable causes when it is obvious what has happened."

"Have it your own way," said Mark indifferently. "But remember this, we saw no signs of enemy action during our search for the guards; we have seen no signs of the enemy at all during the patrol and…"

"Hold it, Cap," interrupted Sam. "I saw something, remember?"

"You thought you saw something," corrected Mark. "I saw no signs when I investigated."

"But you could have missed the sign," insisted Sam. "Or maybe they didn't make any. We don't, why should they?"

"It's the guards which worry me," said CarL "I simply can't understand why, if they aren't dead or prisoner, they didn't wait for us. With all due respect, Captain, their absence doesn't make sense if the camp was destroyed other than by enemy action."

"I disagree," said Mark, and despite himself glanced at his chronometer. "It makes very good sense. You have both forgotten that it is almost sunrise."

* * * *

The moon is too cold at night -240 F., but cold can be combated with electrical heating. The moon is too hot during the day, 220 F., and so far no method had been found to refrigerate a pressure suit. Once every fourteen Earth-days the Terminator swept around the moon, turning night into day and day back into night again. At night the patrols ventured out into the coldness but as day hit went underground, resting in the camps and bases and, aside from the essential guards hiding in the shadows, no one ventured out.

It was simple, common sense survival logic that the three guards, if alive, would have headed for the safety of the intermediate base camp as fast as they could.

If they were alive. Mark doubted it and, as they wended their way from the ruined place that they had thought of as home, his mind toyed with the alternative possibilities. The accident, if it had been an accident, could have happened during guard-change. Regulations stated that the guards should remain on duty until relieved but discipline had softened with the lack of any concrete evidence of the enemy and it was possible that one group waited for the other to return before starting out.

Or maybe the explosion had thrown them into craters. Or perhaps it had been a double explosion, the first minor and the second occurring when the guards had returned to give what aid they could. Perhaps, had they stayed, they would have found the torn and mangled remnants of their bodies but Mark hadn't permitted any waste of time. The camp was dead and everyone in it. Colonel Westerlain, Latimer, Blanchard, all the twenty-seven others of the garrison, all gone as if they had never been. They were dead and this was no time for mourning.

The path Mark has chosen wound around the edges of a vast crater before climbing to the summit of the ringing mountains. The going wasn't easy, the rock, rotten with constant temperature changes, threatened to crumble underfoot, and trained caution still dictated that they should leave no footprints or signs of their passage. The distance was ten miles, on Earth a few hours' marching, on the moon despite the low gravity, it took as many hours and the first climb had left them exhausted.

"I can't take much more of this." Sarn, his voice distorted by the conducting helmets, was obviously suffering. Too many cigarettes, too little exercise while in camp, too great attention to self-comfort had softened him. Carl seemed to be in no better shape.

"Can we rest, Captain?" His breathing was laboured. Mark tried to see his features through the viewport but could only catch a glimpse of a vague blur.

"We'll rest for a while." Deliberately Mark didn't give a set time. Relaxation was important to rest and no one could really relax while watching a clock. He settled himself against the rock, the others close to him, their helmets touching his and each other's in a strange intimacy.

"How long, Cap? Before we make Marigold?" Sam coughed the sound echoing from the globular helmet.

"Quite a while yet." Mark didn't want to think about it.

"How long?" Sam was insistent.

"We'll know when we get there." As ever, Carl was practical "Worrying about it won't make the journey any easier."

"I wasn't talking to you," said Sam. "I was talking to the boss man. How long will it be, Cap?"

"I don't know," confessed Mark. "It depends on how we progress, what detours we have to make. Marigold is about a hundred miles from the camp on the same line of latitude toward the dark side. More than that I can't tell you."

"Why not?" Sam was bitter. "It's our neck as well as yours isn't it? Why shouldn't we know the way as well as you?"

It was logical, put like that, as logical as the security measure which had restricted the knowledge of the location of the intermediate base to officers only. Even that knowledge was sketchy, Colonel Westerlain had once pointed to a spot on a map, drawn in a rough circle with his finger, and announced that, in case of emergency, Marigold would be found in that area. Mark, together with the other officers, memorised what seemed to be the easiest route.

"It's in case we get taken prisoner," said Carl, defending Mark before he had a chance to defend himself. "What we don't know we can't talk about."

"And what if something happens to him?" Sam was, as usual, concerned wholly with his, own welfare. "What then? Do we just wander around like a couple of lost sheep?"

"Cut it out," said Mark. "I'm still with you."

"Now you are, but what if…"

"Cut it out!" Deliberately Mark moved from the community of helmets, not wanting to argue and not wanting to create more unpleasantness than already existed. A good officer knows the value of letting his men blow off steam and vent their grievances on their own. His motives, naturally, were misunderstood.

"Toffee-nosed swine." Sam glared through his viewport to where the captain sat alone. "Trust officers to look after themselves."

"Nothing wrong with the captain." Carl instinctively defended the class to which he aspired. "The trouble with you, Sam, is that you don't understand military organisation. An officer is always sent outside with the men; he has to take care of them and they have to take care of him. What sort of army would we have if everyone gave the orders?"

"What happens to us if anything happens to him?" Sam returned to the main question. "Do you know the way to Marigold? You know that you don't and neither do I." It was impossible to get any closer to Carl but Sam's voice suggested that he had managed the impossible. "Say, how about making him tell us? Draw a map or something?"

"You can't make officers do anything they don't want to do. If you try it then that is mutiny. You get shot for mutiny." Carl's tone left no doubt that he would refuse to discuss the matter further. Sam grunted, twisted his head and found the mouthpiece of his water container. He took a long drink of brackish water and suddenly thought of something else.

"Say, how long can we live in these suits?"

Mark was thinking the same thing.

* * * *

A pressure suit was designed to protect life in the vacuum, while allowing the maximum amount of mobility and little else. The protection was provided by insulation and a sealed air unit; mobility by limb-hugging plastic and certain other devices, such as the heating units, were provided to enable the wearer to perform his duties rather than with any object of comfort. Aside from the radio and instruments the suits held three containers. One contained a quart of brackish water and was coupled to a mouth-tube. The others were tongue-operated dispensers, one containing glucose tablets, the other a combination of tranquillisers and pain relievers in capsule form.

Theoretically, a man could live in a pressure suit until he died from thirst but the actual tolerance limit was much less than that. The suits were uncomfortable, the psychological factor was on a mounting curve and the normal maximum time for a man to wear a suit on outside duty was fifteen hours. Mark and his patrol had already been in their suits for twenty-five.

He thought about it, sitting with his back against a rock, staring down the side of the mountain they had climbed with so much effort. They had arrived within sight of the camp twelve hours after the start of their patrol. Three hours had been consumed in reaching the site, the slow and cautious search for the guards, while another ten had been swallowed by their journey. Marigold was, at the least, ninety miles away, say ninety hours to play it safe. That would make at least four, maybe five days in the suits. How long can a man last on a quart of water?

Conditioned reflex made Mark lick his lips. As yet thirst was no problem but he had forgotten how often he had sipped at his container and had no way of knowing how much water remained. The drugs would help, he supposed, at least they were supplied to relieve suit-fatigue and ease minor but irritating physical pain.

Thinking about it started an itch between his shoulder blades and, as if hi sympathy, a chafed spot on his leg reminded him of its presence. Irritably he nudged the heat-control with his chin, turning it down a notch, then, as the itch increased, turned it down even lower. A helmet clanged against his own and Carl's voice can thinly to his ears.

"Shall we make a start, Captain?"

"In a moment." Mark felt a strange reluctance to leave. It was good just to rest, to let the ache fade from his limbs, to sit and stare at the swollen, misty ball of the Earth as it floated in the black sky. He wondered how many people were, at this moment staring up at the Man in the Moon and how many of them, if any, could ever guess that he was the man they were looking at.

"Captain!" Carl's voice held urgency. "Captain, are you all right?"

"Of course." Mark felt irritation and realised, with a start that he had been on the verge of falling asleep. "Have you checked each other's suits?"

"Our equipment is in order, Captain." Again the subtle impatience as if Carl were telling him that he should have known better than to ask.

"Check them again, mine too." Mark rose to his feet, momentarily losing contact, then regaining it with a ring of metal. "Watch for chafes, half-rips, rubbed spots, you know the drill. We had a rough passage up the side of this mountain, and we don't want any accidents;"

"No, sir." Carl registered his acceptance of authority. "If you win please turn around, sir."

Mark grimaced but shuffled around while Carl checked his suit, then did the same in return. He found a rubbed place and applied a self-seal patch, making no comment but knowing that Carl would recognise the lesson. Trust no one, not even yourself. He contacted for a final word before tackling the descent.

"We can't afford to waste any time," he said. "But we don't have to act like fools. We want to arrive, remember that, and the one sure way of not doing it is to take too many chances. We'll stay close to each other on the downward journey and use the rifles as life-lines. Questions?"

"How about radio silence?" The question, from Carl, was surprising. He qualified it, hastily. "Among these peaks there is little chance of our broadcasts being picked up, the rock will act as a barrier."

"It can act as a reflector too," reminded Mark. "We keep radio silence as far as possible. Sam?"

"Why don't you tell us how to get where we're going?" He sounded aggrieved. "If..." He broke off, abruptly, his helmet lifting from contact and Mark caught a glimpse of his face, vague behind the viewport but recognisably tense. He turned to follow Sam's line of vision and then, suddenly, knew what had caused him to linger at the top of the mountain. He saw the dawning of a new Lunar day.

It was a beautiful sight and one which, in other circumstances, he would have enjoyed. In the far distance, across the bowl of the plain, the tips of jagged peaks glowed fire and gold with the eye-searing brilliance of the naked Sun. Even as he watched the line of light came closer, sliding down the nearside slopes of the mountains, reaching forward as if eager to catch up with the three men.

"God!" It was Sam, radio silence forgotten. "We'll never make it!"

"Steady!" Mark could feel, his stomach tightening at the sight but knew that panic was useless. "We'll be in the shadow going down and, with luck, may even make it over the next range. Wait!" He shouted the word as the others left him. "Sam! Carl! Take it easy!" He was wasting his time and he knew it. The sight of the dawn had brought fear, and panic was in command as the two men raced away from the advancing line of light. Then, despite himself, panic caught Mark too and he joined the others in their headlong dash down the crumbling, slopes.

It was a nightmare journey down treacherous slopes and precipitous walls of stone. They ignored the elements of personal safety, poising to spring out and down, drifting in the low gravity to land, their metal soled boots scrabbling, to poise and spring again. Once Mark felt himself slipping sideways, toppling slowly down towards a place where up-thrust spurs of stone waited to impale him like blunt knives or smash his helmet with clubs of granite. Desperately he fought to regain his balance, succeeding at the cost of a wrenched ankle, ignoring the sudden stab of pain as he continued his headlong flight. Twice Sam fell, both times leaping to his feet, the luck which always seems to attend fools strong with him. On the lower slopes Carl, who had moved with inborn grace, misjudged and landed heavily on his side, rolling, the clatter of his helmet echoing from the radio. Mark reached him, knelt by his side and anxiously examined the precious air unit. It was dented but appeared unharmed.

"How are you, Carl?"

"Shaken, but that's about all." Carl struggled to his feet. "Where's Sam?"

"Well ahead of us." Mark glanced towards the running figure. Sam had reached the plain and was racing along the edge of the dust-filled crater. "He'll be all right. Do you want to rest for a while?"

"No, sir." Already Carl was moving. "We can't afford to waste time." Abruptly he broke into a run and the mad, use-less race against time was on again.

And it was a useless race, Mark knew that even as he ran in the path Sam had made: Before them reared a second ridge of towering peaks and beyond that would be a third, a fourth and then a long, low, exposed section of rock, over which they had to pass. Long before they reached that rock the Lunar day would have caught up with them. Fast as they were moving it was impossible for them to move faster than the advancing line of heat and light. But Mark hoped that, at least, they would make it over the next ridge.

It wasn't too hard a climb, on Earth an Alpine Club would have made easy work of it, but hampered by the suits, sweat-ing and exhausted from their insane dash down the far ridge and across: the plain, it taxed their strength to the uttermost.

Sam went first, living proof of how panic can lend a man unaccustomed strength. Carl followed a close second, while Mark toiled at the rear. All of them, at one point or another, had lost or discarded their weapons.

Despite himself Mark kept twisting his body so as to look backwards. He wasted time by performing the manoeuvre but he couldn't help it. He felt like a man running from an enemy or as if he were living a nightmare in which he ran and ran and yet didn't seem to move. But this was no nightmare and the enemy was very real.

The enemy was the dawn and the more than 400 degrees difference of temperature which would come with it. Once in the light of the naked Sun his suit would be heated from well below zero to above the boiling point of water. The plastic could stand; the temperature range and the material was a poor conductor, but even so life would rapidly became unbearable.

A man is, at all times, generating heat. Normally that heat is dispersed by conduction, convection and radiation. You can't lose heat other than by radiation while in a vacuum and, though heat could be lost by direct contact with the surface of the moon that became impossible as soon as the immediate temperature, rose higher than that of the suit. Inevitably the outside heat would penetrate, the suit, adding to the bodily generated temperature of the wearer. And no man can live for long at a temperature higher than that of boiling water.

The sunrise moved fast, too fast. Mark stared at its rapid advance, each time the sight spurring him to greater effort. The gleaming, light slid down the far slope, stole relentlessly over the plain and drew an advancing line of brightness beneath his feet. It caught up with him when he was almost at the summit of the ridge.

It was as if a light of intense brilliance had suddenly blazed on his back, pinning him to the rock as if he were a fly caught in the beam of a powerful searchlight. Reflections from the stone dazzled his eyes so that he moved, lids half-closed, fumbling for hand- and foot-holds, feeling his way to the top and the cold, dark safety of the shadows on the other side.

"Captain!" Carl ignored the radio silence. "Are you all right?"

It was a stupid question, Mark felt as if he were being boiled. Gasping, he turned his head until his mouth found the water tube. Greedily he sucked and then, remembering, spat out the mouth piece. "Sam?"

"There." Carl pointed down the ridge. "He didn't stop."

"Crazy idiot!" Mark felt a quick anxiety. "Sam! Sam, do you hear me? Slow down, you fool, you'll kill yourself!"

If Sam heard he made no answer, but the sound of his breathing, harsh and laboured, almost sobbing as it came over the radio, was answer enough. He was a man crazed with fear and the fear was contagious.

"Let's go." Carl sprang down to a lower section of the ridge. "Let's get moving before the sunlight catches us."

"It's caught us already." Mark had to restrain himself from repeating his wild passage down the first ridge. Luck had been with him then, it might not be with him a second time. He caught up with Carl and grabbed his arm. "Take it easy."

"We can't waste time!" Carl's breath, like Sam's, like Mark's own, sobbed in his throat. "We've got to keep moving."

"We need to rest." Mark knew that he couldn't continue the too-rapid pace much longer. Fatigue was blinding him to danger and, sooner or later, he would take a false step and plunge to his death. He dug his fingers hard into the plastic covering Carl's arm. "That's an order! Understand?"

For a moment Carl's panic struggled with his innate desire to obey, then, just as panic was winning, Sam missed his footing.

He gave a half-grunt, half-curse then, as he toppled over a sheer drop, their helmets rang to his screams. He took a long time falling, drifting down with the casual, deceptively gentle motion of a low gravity world, but when he hit his inertia was high and his screams died with the impact.

Mark was thankful for that; when a man has to die it is best that he die quickly.

* * * *

The cave was a small hollow scooped in the side of the mountain. Inside it was dark with perpetual shadow, not even the earthlight ever penetrating more than a little way past the opening. From the mouth of the cave it was possible to look down over the foothills, over the vast, dust-filled crater and on to where the ring-mountains reached for the sky. Mark sat and stared at the distant ridge, his mouth still furry from sleep, his head aching and his body throbbing from his recent exertions. Behind him, sprawled on the floor, Carl rested in uneasy slumber.

Mark could tell it was uneasy from the sounds echoing from his radio. The breathing was ragged, broken, more like the breathing of a man who has run hard and fought harder than that of a man in the last stages of sleep. But sleep, any sleep, was escape from the torment of the suits.

Outside the mountains and plain scintillated with sun-glare, the sunrise had caught and passed them long ago. Some-where on the upper slopes Sam rested in final dissolution; they had not troubled to find and hide his body. The journey downward had been a horror of light and shadow, the contrast between the illuminated sections and the midnight shadow making each stage of the journey a progress into potential oblivion. They had found the cave and almost immediately fallen into exhausted slumber. Now, awake, Mark had time for thought and worry, thought, for planning and decision. A catch in the breathing and a low mumble warned him that Carl was finally awake.

"Captain! Where are you, Captain?"

"Here." Mark withdrew into the cave and knelt beside his companion. "Relax, Carl, everything is under control."

"Yes, sir." The sounds of restless moving and a liquid gurgling.

"Better take it easy on the water, Carl. We're going to need every drop."

"Yes, sir." Carl's voice was mechanical. "Just a little to rinse out my mouth." He stirred, rested his hands beside him and heaved himself upright. "God! My head!"

"Take a couple of drug tablets." Mark had already taken half of his. "Some glucose, too; we burned a lot of energy coming over the mountains."

"Yes, sir." Again the mechanical acceptance of higher authority. Mark stared through the viewport but in the darkness could see nothing.

"Are you all right, Carl?"

"My head's killing me." The sound of sucking as he helped himself to a sweet. "Sorry, sir, to be this way. I'll get over it."

"Of course you will." Mark forced a cheerfulness he did not feel into his voice. "Air supply all right?"

"I think so, sir. Nothing I can do about it if it isn't, is there?"

"No," said Mark evenly, "there isn't. But don't worry about it."

Carl wasn't worrying, Mark knew that. Exhaustion coupled with shock had driven him into a temporary retreat. He was a natural-born soldier and automatically he had thrown all the necessity for making decisions on to his officer. Mark, to him, was now father and God. What he ordered Carl would do, mechanically unthinkingly, more like a robot than a man. It was a state of mind Mark hoped he would soon recover from.

"I've been thinking of a plan of action," he said. "Actually we've no great problem. Our big enemy is the sun-glare but the suits can stand brief exposures without overheating and we stand good chance. We'll make the journey in short stages, finding cover in shadows when we get too hot." He waited for comment. "Carl?"

"Yes, Captain?"

"Any suggestions? Questions? Anything to add?"

"How about the viewports?" Carl stirred and his voice took on fresh interest. "The glare is pretty bad, sir, can we dim them in some way?"

"None that I can see. These suits were designed for earth-light conditions and sun-filters weren't included." Privately, Mar cursed those responsible for the specifications of the suits. Weight and cost, of course, the two important essentials, with cost taking high priority.

"How long do you think it will take. Captain?"

"Not too long." Mark drew lines in the thin film of dust before the mouth of the cave. "Here was the camp." He traced a path. "This is the first range and this the second." His finger jabbed a small clearing. "We're about here. Now Marigold lies over here, say about eighty miles, maybe less. We've to cross two more ranges, small ones and then a long ridge of rock. Nothing to it, normally, and we've passed the hardest part." His flattened hand obliterated the crude map. "Just keep heading directly away from the Sun and you'll come to it."

Carl grunted, suit-terminology for a nod.

"Now follow me closely." Mark hunched himself to the edge of light entering the cave. "We'll make for that ledge, there should be a shadow-patch under it. Then we'll cross over to that crevasse and after that backtrack to that broken ground. One long stage will take us to the plain and there should be some shadow under those boulders. Another long stage over to the foothills and then up the ridge from cave-to cave. We'll have to find them as we go, I can't spot any from here. Half-way up we'll swing right through that shallow pass." Mark dropped his arm. "Just stay close to me and we'll be all right."

"I hope so." Carl made a choking sound. "Sorry, Captain, but it's my head. Shall we go now?"

"Yes." Mark rose and then, like a swimmer taking the plunge, stepped out into the brilliant sun-glare. It was like stepping into a furnace.

It wasn't the heat—that would come later when his body began to perspire and the air grow hot to his lungs, it was the glare. The fury of the naked sun reflected back from scabrous rock and volcanic dust, shimmering as it struck his viewport and seeming to penetrate his eyes until it rested on the surface of his brain. And there was no escaping the glare.

Mark tried. He accelerated his pace, memorising little stretches of the path and following them with his eyes closed. He tried bending at the waist but then lost the blackness of the sky. He tried turning his head but met tiny suns shining from the coverings of his instruments. The only real escape was speed; the only real surcease the brief respite of the shadows.

It was cat and mouse with the ever-watchful Sun as the cat and Mark and Carl as the frenzied, scampering mice. Darkness spelt safety; light spelt discomfort and eventual death. So they raced from the cave to the ledge and rested until their breath eased in their lungs and their hearts slowed their pounding. They raced from the ledge to the crevasse and found no shadow so ran over to the broken ground where they crawled into midnight black like nocturnal insect seeking shelter. Then the long torture to the boulders on the plain, the longer torture to the foothills and the scramble up the ridge until they found the sanctuary of a cave.

And when they found it Mark discovered that Carl was dying.

* * * *

It was the air-unit, and he had been afraid of what might happen all along. The units were tested to twenty-four hours and they had been in the suits for three times longer than that. And Carl had damaged his unit when he had fallen on the journey down the first ridge. Subconsciously Mark had been expecting trouble, consciously he had tried to forget it, but now it had to be faced.

"It's my head, Captain," Carl said. His tone was diffident as if he were apologising for something he should have been able to avoid. "I'm hot and I can't seem to breathe and my head is killing me."

"Take some drugs." It was poor advice but all Mark could offer.

"I've taken the drugs, Captain, all of them, the water too but it doesn't seem to help." Carl lifted his gloved hands and pressed them over his viewport. "If I could only cut down the glare, maybe that would help."

Mark didn't answer, he sat, feeling his stomach tighten, waiting for what he knew had to come.

"Could it be the air-unit, Captain?" At last Carl had managed to face it. "I had a pretty bad fall and maybe it got thrown out of kilter. I remember what they told us back at school, about the air units I mean, could that be the trouble, Captain?"

"Steady." Mark had caught the warning note of hysteria "No need for panic, Carl. I'll take a look."

It was a gesture and both of them knew it. It was impossible for the wearer of a suit to reach his own air-unit. He couldn't even open his helmet, nor could he shed the suit un-aided. A man in suit was a helpless prisoner in a personal cell, totally dependent on others to restore him back to a natural life. Mark could see Carl's unit, could touch it and superficially examine it, but that was all. He had neither the tools nor skill to effect repairs and, even if he had, they would have been useless in a vacuum. If Carl's unit was faulty then Carl was going to die.

"I can't see anything wrong." Mark gently ran his hands over the connections from upper shoulders to helmet. "It's possible that the fall upset the CO_2 regulator. Excessive carbon dioxide would account for the shortness of breath and the headache. At the rate we've been operating you need plenty of oxygen and you may not have been getting it." He ran his fingers over the slight dent he had discovered in the tough metal. "Maybe the humidity control is out of action too, but that isn't important." He tried to sound cheerful. "Never mind. Carl, we'll be at Marigold before things get too serious."

"I don't think that I can make it to Marigold, Captain." Carl paused, gasping for breath. "I don't think that I can go much further, not the way things are."

"Nonsense!" Mark was brusque. "That's no way for a soldier to talk, Carl. I thought that you were tough."

"I thought so too, but I've never been this long in a suit before." Carl twisted his body so that he stared at the brilliance outside the cave. "I'm sorry, Captain, but I can't take much more of it. I feel closed in, buried alive, just as if I were a man in a coffin." He gave a bitter chuckle. "I am too, am I not?"

"Only if you want to be." Mark tried to see the other's face but the reflected light obscured the viewport. "A man can keep going just as long as he wants to, Carl. It's only when he gives in that he's beaten. So we've been a long time in the suits and by the time we reach Marigold we'll have probably set a record, but that's no reason to think we can't do it. We can do it and we will do it—if we want to."

"If we are able to, Captain," corrected Carl. "A man can't walk if he can't breathe."

"You're assuming things, Carl. We don't know that your unit is faulty. You feel weak and out of breath but that could be due to other causes. Suit-fatigue, an upset stomach, a developing chill, almost anything. Don't let your mind trick you into giving up when there is no real cause for it." Mark forced confidence into his voice. "We'll make it, Carl, both of us and you know what? When we reach Marigold I'm recommending you for a commission. Isn't that worth trying for?"

"I'd like a commission," said Carl. "Thank you, sir, I appreciate your good intentions."

"I'm selfish," said Mark. "I want to be on the winning side of this war and one way to do it is to select good men for command positions."

"Yes, sir." Carl was silent for a long time, so long that Mark thought he had fallen asleep. "You know, Captain. I've been thinking. All the time I've been on the moon I've never killed an enemy. That's what a soldier is for, isn't it. Captain, to kill the enemy. I've never done that. That sort of makes me a bad soldier, doesn't it?"

"You and me both," said Mark. It was a subject he didn't want to talk about. "Better get some rest now, Carl, we've a hard time ahead of us."

"But the enemy has killed us. Captain." Carl seemed determined to pursue his train of thought. "They destroyed the camp and wiped out the guards. They really killed Sam; if they hadn't blown up the camp he wouldn't have died. And they are going to get us too, in the end."

"How?" Mark yawned, he was having difficulty in staying awake, despite the discomfort of the suit. "Because we might not make it to Marigold, you mean?"

"Maybe we won't be allowed to make it much further." Carl's voice lost itself in introspection. "We've grown careless, Captain, what with forgetting to set a rear guard and not watching and not being too careful about the tracks we're leaving behind us. If they were out there we'd be easy to follow."

"If they were out in the sunlight they'd be roasting in their suits," said Mark. "They'd have more to worry about than us." He yawned again. "Get some sleep, Carl."

"I'm not tired, sir. Have you considered the possibility…"

"That's enough!" Mark was tired and had no intention of pandering to Carl's morbid line of thought. "There's no one out there and, if there were, then you're doing the worst thing possible by not maintaining radio silence. Now quit worrying about nothing and get some rest. That's an order!"

"Yes, sir." Carl didn't alter his position. "Captain?"

"What is it now?" Mark was impatient.

"You'll get to Marigold, sir. You don't have to worry."

Mark didn't reply. Deliberately he switched off his radio and, sprawling on the floor of the cave, closed his eyes and tried for sleep. Despite his physical exhaustion sleep did not come easily, nerves were too strained to immediately relax and he felt a touch of guilt at having been so curt. Carl was a dying man. He should be gentle with him, understanding, perhaps he could even find some way to fool destiny and get them both safely to Marigold. When he awoke he would think about it.

But when he awoke Mark was alone.

* * * *

There is no place lonelier than the face of a dead world. Space is lonely but space has never known life and it is so vast, so impersonal, that loneliness becomes transmuted into awe. But a dead world is like a graveyard; full of ghosts and memories of what it might have been and, to a solitary man, the endless stretches of barrenness begin to take on a dreadful menace.

Mark began to feel that menace as if the moon were a vindictive thing; a mass of deadness intent on destroying the single speck of life which crawled and ran, scampered and stumbled over its serrated face. In the heavens, the Sun glowed with the imaginary fires of Hell and the Earth, pale in comparison, seemed almost like the figment of a dream.

"Stop it!" Mark shook his head in the confines of the helmet, hardly aware that he was speaking to himself. "You've only one aim in life, boy, and that's to get to Marigold and do it fast." Automatically his mouth found the water tube. Sucking was a waste of time, the container was empty, but sucking produced a little saliva which eased his burning throat. He felt resentment that he couldn't lick the perspiration from his body, his suit was clammy with sweat and his thirst was so great that liquid, in any form, would have been welcome.

"Got to get moving." He forced himself from the patch of shadow and stumbled, no longer able to run, towards another tiny oasis of darkness. Despite himself he began to think of Carl.

He should have known what the other had intended, the clues had been obvious, even to the position Carl had adopted in the cave, almost as if he were a self-appointed guard. And his talk of the enemy, it all added up. Wrong, of course, but to a man suffering from suit-fatigue anything could be made logical and nothing was impossible.

Carl had convinced himself that the enemy had been re-sponsible for the destruction of the camp. That they had done it with a cunning purpose and that they had followed the sur-viving patrol. The reason? Because they wanted to be guided to Marigold, there to repeat their symphony of destruction. It would be a victory, if they could blast the intermediate camp. Not a decisive victory, of course, but a victory all the same. And so Carl, poor deluded fool, had walked out of the cave and taken up the rear guard, determined to prove himself a soldier by killing a non-existent enemy, sacrificing himself so that Mark could make his way to safety with a clear con-science.

"Nuts," said Mark to himself. "The guy was as batty as a bat. Crazy!" He stumbled, tried to save himself and fell, rolling awkwardly and screaming with pain as the Sun lanced through his viewport, seeming to sear through his lids to char his eyes. On his feet once again he blinked to try to dear away the retinal image and, because of the flaring spots of red and green filling his eyes, tripped and fell again. This time he took longer to regain his feet.

"Getting weak," he mumbled. "If anyone's following me they'd have an easy time." He gave a chuckle. "Following me! Who the hell'd want to be out in this weather?" Then, suddenly, it wasn't a joke any more.

It was a little thing which jerked him back to sanity, noth-ing but a footprint in the dust. It was one of a dozen leading from one bare stretch of rock to another, long, broad oblongs, the marks made by booted feet. And, staring at them, Mark felt Carl's suspicions rear in his own mind with a horrible clarity.

How long ago the marks had been made it was impossible to tell. A mark on the Luna dust stayed there until obliterated by artificial means. Given long enough the natural crumbling of the rock would tend to soften the outlines but no one knew how long that would take. Without air there could be no wind and changes, caused by alterations of temperature in the absence of water, were slow. The marks could have been made ten years earlier, during the past night or the night before that, or they could have been made in the past ten minutes. Mark couldn't tell and he had no way of ever finding out. But one thing was certain. Men had made those marks. And the moon held two kinds of men.

Just where he was Mark didn't know but he could be somewhere near Marigold. The marks might have been made by members of the garrison or by an earlier expedition. Equally, they could have been made by the enemy. If made by the enemy then they could be hiding somewhere this very moment, watching, waiting for him to lead them to the intermediate base. Mark had no proof either way, only knowledge, and it was the knowledge which gripped the pit of his stomach and set his heart pounding.

The knowledge that, if the marks had been made by the enemy then the one thing he dared not do was to lead them any further And he had to assume that they had been made by the enemy.

The Sun was as bright as ever as he slowly moved away but he did not look towards the Sun. Instead he looked up at the Earth, so misty and unreal, so beautiful as it hung glowing in the sky. It would t cool on the Earth, with soft winds and rain and the scent of growing things. He began to walk towards it, moving away from where Marigold might be, his head filled with, dreams.

Dreams of a triumphal return with himself as a hero. Visions of a long, lazy holiday at the Polar resort where he would be surrounded with crisp, cold ice and snow, where he could bath in icy water and gulp gallons of ice cream and chilled white wine. A wonderful dream of contentment and an earthly paradise.

And one which would never be soured by the touch of reality.

ABOUT THE AUTHOR

English writer E. C. Tubb is internationally known, having been translated into more than a dozen languages. In a sixty-year writing career he published over 120 novels, and more than 200 science fiction short stories in such magazines as *Astounding/Analog*, *Authentic*, *Fantasy Adventures*, *Galaxy*, *Nebula*, *New Worlds*, *Science Fantasy*, and *Vision of Tomorrow*.

Tubb's early science fiction novels were exciting adventure stories, written in the prevailing fashion of the early 1950s. Yet, from his very first novel, his work was characterized at all times by a sense of plausibility, logic, and human insight. These qualities were even more evident in his short stories, which were frequently anthologized.

By 1956 his output included adventure, detective stories, and westerns, but he remained best known for his numerous science fiction novels, of which *Alien Dust* (1955) and *The Space Born* (1956) were acknowledged classics. Tubb became famous for his long-running "Dumarest of Terra" series of novels, the galaxy-spanning saga of Earl Dumarest and his search to find his way back across the stars to the legendary lost planet where he was born—Earth. They eventually spanned thirty-three titles, the final one, *Child of Earth*, appearing in November 2008. Equally well known were his *Space 1999* TV novelizations, and his "Cap Kennedy" novels. Some of his finest SF short stories were collected in *The Best Science Fiction of E. C. Tubb* (Wildside, 2003). Tubb continued to write dynamic science fiction novels right up to his death in October, 2010.